THINGS CHANGE

By

Michie Gibson

Published by T & M Creations, LLC
@2019 Michie Gibson

ACKNOWLEDGEMENTS

A Huge Thank You to the following:

Lindsey Moreland for all your help and guidance, I can never thank you enough.

My beta and proof readers, Candi Lyons, Carol Holmes, Vaughn Gibson and David Bryson.

My good friends, Randy Fowler, a retired homicide detective, and Bob Lyons, a retired Police Lieutenant, for offering me guidance on police procedures, advice which I may or may not have taken.

My life long and best friend, William Harris, who did not give me permission to use his name and about whom I made up a lot of shit.

And, Last but not Least, I want to thank my wife, Theresa, for always being there for me.

DISCLAIMER:

This is a work of fiction. Names, characters, businesses, places, events, locales, and incidents are either the products of the author's imagination or used in a fictitious manner. Any resemblance to actual persons, living or dead, or actual events is purely coincidental.

CHAPTER 1

*T*hings change. The weather had changed abruptly in Nashville, Tennessee. It's February and the weather is unseasonably warm. The traffic is unusually heavy for this time of day, but that's ok I've got a lot to think about on my short drive.

I received my first large fee as an attorney and I'm on my way to Harding Place CCA, a private Correctional Institution, to visit my new client. Probably a better way to look at it is that my new client's mother paid me my first big retainer. Although I am thirty-eight years old, I don't have an established practice like most attorneys my age. I've only been practicing law a couple of years and have been surviving mostly by appointments from Judge Sheila Calloway and representing clients that are divorcing but can hardly afford an attorney up until this point. Not that it's a bad living. I'm making more money than I had a few years back working for Billy Burns in his illicit after hour's club, Sherry's.

Billy was a well-known character around Nashville. He had been around town a long time, and knew how to cultivate the right kind of friends. Over the years, he had provided services for judges, politicians and high-ranking police officials. These longtime friends allowed Billy to run his operation while they looked the other way.

I view the two occupations, working for Billy at Sherry's and practicing law, as adventures.

Since becoming an attorney, Judge Calloway has taken me under her wing and appointed me cases. Taking an appointed case is something most attorneys don't want to do. Appointed cases are cases for which attorneys are paid by the state to represent indigent defendants, or people who can't afford an attorney. The pay wasn't great, but it wasn't that bad either. Those checks from the Administrative Office of the Courts can keep you afloat. In truth, there are attorneys who never do anything but take appointed cases.

I never wanted to live on appointed cases alone and am grateful for this fee to come my way. Might as well admit it, I didn't become an attorney because I wanted to better humanity. I became an attorney because I wanted to make a living doing something not everyone could do. The same reason I jumped at the opportunity to work for Billy in the after-hours club years ago.

Sherry's was located at the entrance to the Fairgrounds on Wedgewood Avenue in Nashville. It was called an after-hours club because it only opened at two o'clock in the morning and closed when the sun came up.

The club did not have a liquor license, but liquor was sold on the premises. Billy skirted that law by calling Sherry's a private club and requiring all of its patrons to have a membership card. He would have the bartenders write customers' names on a piece of tape and stick the tape to the bottles of liquor behind the bar. That way he could tell the Alcohol Firearms & Tobacco agents, who came around from time to time, that the bottles belonged to the club members and he just charged them for serving the drinks. Everyone knew this was a farce. As a matter of fact, my only criminal conviction is for bootlegging, a charge I pleaded guilty to one of the times Sherry's was raided by the police and he needed someone to take a charge to get the heat off him.

In truth, Sherry's was a popular hangout for bartenders and servers who worked in clubs that were legit but had to close at two in the morning. Sherry's was also frequented by politicians, police officers and the occasional low-level gangster. It was a good mix. The patrons there liked to think they were special because we didn't allow everyone in the club.

To get into Sherry's, you had to know somebody. That's

where I came in. Security was my responsibility, along with my longtime friend Dakota Gray. Dakota had been my best friend for many years and still is to this day.

Our duties at Sherry's were varied. When the club was open, we would take turns standing at the front door, or walking through the club to make sure everything was running smoothly. The front door was a heavy thick door with a peep hole, like you would see in movies. When someone knocked on the door, we would slide the peep hole open and decide whether they were welcome or not. We used to refer to ourselves as maintenance. In short, our objective was to keep the place clean and, when needed, take out the trash

Billy also owned the residential house that was right next door to Sherry's. He converted the three-bedroom house into a casino. The living room had a round poker table sitting in the middle of the room with eight chairs for the poker players. Directly behind the table there were couches pushed up against the wall for the girlfriends of the gamblers to hang out and watch the game. The kitchen had been converted into a fully stocked bar with a buffet set up for the gamblers and their guests. The bedrooms were used by the gamblers and their girlfriends when they needed to take a break from the action before getting back into the game.

Sherry's was closed Sunday through Tuesday. That's when Billy used the house next door to run high stakes poker games for high rollers. To get into the game you had to buy a minimum of twenty-five thousand dollars in chips. Depending on how many gamblers were involved, there could be hundreds of thousands of dollars in the house. As security, our duty on those nights was to sit shotgun on the game and make sure no one was enough of an idiot to try and rob the game.

There had been two such idiots over the years. Dakota caught one of them trying to jimmy the back door. The would-be robber was able to get in the door, but quickly regretted his decision when he found Dakota waiting for him on the other side. The second idiot tried to rob the game on my watch. He made it all the way to the poker room and demanded all the money at gun point, however, he didn't see me and I had the angle on him so I was able to pull my pistol and put it to the back of his head. I cocked the pistol and said in a quiet tone of voice, "I can promise you the only way you get to live tonight is if you drop that gun." He dropped the gun and immediately started begging for mercy. We didn't hurt either one of those guys, we just let them go. Word was out on the street - our game was not to be fucked with.

Dakota and I made extra money at the club by selling pot, or marijuana, out the back door. One of us would work the back door while the other one was working the front door. Billy knew we were dealing, but he didn't care, so long as our side business didn't cause him any trouble.

Billy actually hooked us up with our supplier, Jack Adams. I never did like Jack. Supplying pot to dealers was not his only business. Jack used the money he made from selling pot to bankroll a loan shark business. Jack became wealthy running these two enterprises. He liked to flaunt his money, and was ruthless when someone didn't pay their debts on time. Jack delighted in sending his thugs to work over the poor slob who couldn't keep their agreement.

Jack asked Dakota and I to work for him collecting bad debts. We both declined. That's not the way we wanted to earn a living.

Besides, the money I made selling pot and working for Billy was more than anything I could have made working in a factory job, which was about all I was qualified to do.

When we were working for Billy, I knew we were breaking the law. Even though we were committing crimes, they were "no harm, no foul" type crimes. No one was supposed to get hurt and I sincerely believed every service we provided should be legal. That's why, back in those days, I likened myself to more of an outlaw than a criminal. Working at Sherry's had been a great adventure to me at first. It just didn't end that way.

Today I am an attorney, with a career changing retainer

in my pocket, on my way to meet a client, John Lester, who is charged with murder. I draw comfort in knowing that my days of being what I like to think of as an "outlaw" are long over.

Six years ago, after I had beaten a murder charge and was free from the worry of going to prison, I decided not to go back to Sherry's. I did stay in the club business working security, but I was out of the pot trade. I decided to re-enroll in college. Working the clubs offered me the ability to earn a decent living at night, and attend class during the day. I wanted to better myself, but didn't want to be dirt poor in the meantime.

I only had one thing on my mind back then. I knew I was going to be an attorney. One day, I told Dakota, "selling pot is like standing in line to go to prison," (After being in jail for ten months, I now know prison was the last place I wanted to be.) I told him "I am going to get out of line and let someone else take my turn." I doubt he'd ever really heard it put that way before. He thought for a moment, then his face broke out in a big grin, and he said, "You're right, I'm going to get out of line too."

After I graduated from Nashville School of Law, I became a member of the bar and a practicing attorney. The cases Judge Calloway appointed me not only kept me fed, but turned out to be high profile cases and I received a lot of media attention. I guess I was lucky. I felt like I had always been lucky. I had successful results in many of those appointed cases and the notoriety started bringing in better paying cases; hence the reason I got this nice fee that I am going to visit John Lester about today.

When I was in law school, Judge Calloway had been the criminal law professor at the Nashville School of Law and was the elected District Attorney for Nashville Davidson County, Tennessee. Even before I went to law school, Judge Calloway had been the D.A. for Nashville and was in charge when I was on trial for murder. Unbeknownst to me, Judge Calloway remembered me from that trial and was impressed that I had turned my life around. I learned later that she had followed my progress and was instrumental in keeping me in law school when I picked up an assault charge during my second year. If it hadn't been for her standing firm with the Dean of the law school, I wouldn't be an attorney today.

John Lester's mother, Ann Lester, told me that he demanded that she hire me as his attorney. She said he wanted me because he read in the paper, how a new attorney won two high profile murder cases in less than a year. In my mind, it never hurts to get media attention. I am sure to get some on this case.

Today is different from times past though, as John Lester is charged with first-degree murder. A few years ago, I was the one sitting in jail waiting to meet with an attorney to discuss a first-degree murder charge. The biggest difference between my case and the one I am going to visit John Lester about today is that he is more than likely facing the death penalty. Our murder cases did certainly have one thing in common though, we both have taken a life, or more than one in his case if the news reports are to be believed.

John Lester is charged with three of the most horrific murders. They are so sadistic in nature, and done with such unimaginable brutality that when reports of the crimes were made public, it rocked the Nashville Community to its core. The murders have been in the local media spotlight for the last sixteen months.

I don't find it particularly distressing that I might be representing a guilty psychopath who is accused of such barbarism. That doesn't concern me. I've always told my clients, and will tell John Lester the same, it doesn't matter to me whether you are guilty or innocent. What matters to me is whether or not the government can prove John Lester is guilty of first-degree murder and, if so, does he deserve the death penalty?

Defending guilty clients is nothing new to me and I reckon John Lester is no exception. If necessary, I will use a previous case to convey to John how I feel about representing a client that I'm pretty confident is guilty of the crimes which they have been accused of committing. It was actually my first ever murder trial. I knew that client was guilty, but the state couldn't prove it. That particular client was found not guilty at trial. I want John to know that if the government can't prove he is guilty, beyond a reasonable doubt, I will fight for an innocent verdict.

That previous case was a gangland killing. Judge Calloway appointed me to represent the defendant whose street name was A.K. A.K. was facing a first-degree murder charge for killing a rival gang member. The government's case rested on witnesses that were homeless drug addicts and some innocent bystanders who were too afraid to come forward and testify. Because of that, the government lost its case and my client, A.K., was acquitted.

I tried that case knowing that A.K. was guilty. That didn't matter to me. What mattered to me was whether or not the government could prove it. The fact that A.K. was found not guilty at trial didn't bother me. Even though that was not what should have happened, it was still justice. Justice dictates that a citizen being charged with a crime must not be found guilty unless there is reasonable evidence that they committed that crime.

In my mind the law is justice. We have a legal system that looks at a disputed issue and listens impartially to the facts and laws that govern and, ideally, reaches the correct conclusion. In this country, one is innocent until proven guilty not the other way around. The government must obey the rule of law and satisfy the burden of proof before it can take a human being's liberty away. I firmly believe that.

Today I find myself hoping the government will have enough proof to put this monster away if he is guilty. I have read the news and know what John Lester is accused of doing. Unfortunately, if the government doesn't have enough proof, then I will have to do what honor dictates I do. The oath I swore when I was admitted to the bar as a practicing attorney demands that I zealously represent my clients to the best of my ability. I will do that. If the government does not have sufficient proof that John Lester is guilty, then I will have to find a way to get the slimy sack of shit off.

Truth is, I am not really worried about whether or not the government has enough evidence to convict John Lester. I feel confident he will have to enter a plea to save his life. Hopefully, I can explain this to John and we can work out a plea. That way I will never have to go to trial with this bastard. In my mind, this would be the best result for everyone. His mother would be grateful he was living. John would be in prison where he couldn't hurt another child. And I would have earned my money and kept my promise to the judicial system.

Unfortunately, the truth is, I'm not confident that John Lester is guilty. I know he is guilty. I spoke to the public defender, Laura Kincaid, who represented John briefly before I was hired. She let me know that he is every bit of guilty. She also let me know that she is scared to death of him. Laura was in the process of asking the court to relieve her as attorney of record before John's mother hired me.

While getting the case files from Laura, she explained to me that John Lester is above average intelligence and is a total psychopath. She was terrified every time she had to visit him in jail. She said, "William, I don't care how much they offer you. Let this one go."

Laura didn't believe John Lester stood a chance of winning a trial by jury. She told me that the government had DNA evidence linking him to the murder of Rebecca Springer. Rebecca was the last girl killed out of the three little girls that had been murdered. Laura also told me that the State only had enough evidence to convict him for the murder of Rebecca Springer. The evidence, Laura claimed, against John for the murders of the other two children is only circumstantial. However, the three murders were so similar in nature that the government went ahead and charged John with all three.

Laura thought the government's plan might be to try John for the murder of Rebecca Springer first and then offer him a plea bargain to save his life if he would plead guilty for the murders of the other two girls. I must admit, I sure hope that is how it works out.

I value her opinion, but I also want the money. The $100,000 retainer, plus the $25,000.00 for expenses John Lester's mother paid me will go a long way towards keeping me on my feet for the next few months. I am not afraid of John Lester, having dealt with more than my fair share of tough characters in my life. On top of that, what could he do? John is locked up with guards all around; it would be hard for him to attack me.

As I drive towards the correctional facility, I find myself daydreaming that if John Lester is guilty, maybe I wouldn't mind him attacking me. That would justify my beating the dog shit out of him and, at the same time, I could probably even keep the fee. The money was paramount in my mind. In my former life, I probably would have beaten the dog shit out of him anyway, but I have to remind myself those days are over. For so many years I was an outlaw. Now as an officer of the court my duty is to uphold the law. But a wise man once said, "old habits die hard".

I picture this case working out like this: If the government has enough proof to convict John Lester of first-degree murder, then I will explain that to him. I will advise him that it might be in his best interest to take a plea. If he doesn't want to take a plea, then he has the constitutional right to a trial by jury. It is his decision if he wants to exercise that right, but I will also tell him, based on the evidence, that he will most likely be found guilty. Doesn't matter to me, either way I will have earned the $100,000 his mother paid me and I will feel good about the system. After all, everyone charged with a crime in our system of justice deserves and has a privilege of having a competent attorney represent them. And in my mind, that's what I am.

At first, I never liked visiting my clients in jail. Too many unhappy memories from my time inside. Over the past couple of years, I have gotten used to it and even enjoy going to visit clients there in some ways. Just as walking in takes me down memory lane, so does walking out. It sure feels good to get to leave when the meetings are over. The next best thing to walking out of that place, is watching someone that I am representing walk out. To me that is the greatest high.

As for John Lester, if the government does have sufficient proof, I feel like it is my responsibility to explain that to him and, if possible, work out a plea bargain with the District Attorney. To be honest, I like negotiating plea bargains more than trying cases. I have already tried enough cases to know that it doesn't matter how confident you are in your facts you never know what a jury will do. In most situations, it's better to control your own fate than let twelve other people choose it for you.

I do understand why people choose to go to trial rather than take a plea agreement. When I was charged with first-degree murder, I refused a plea agreement and took my case to trial. It wasn't the most intelligent decision I've ever made, but sometimes fortune favors the bold.

Since avoiding a murder conviction and becoming an attorney, I have taken a sacred oath to protect the Constitution and obey the law of the land. I know I'll never be a crooked attorney, nor will I do anything illegal. Those days are over. That is why I can tell myself that if John Lester is guilty and the government can't prove it, then he needs to walk. No matter what the truth is. On the other hand, if he is guilty and I have to try this case, the system works if the jury finds him guilty because the government has the facts to prove it. Either way, I won't let it bother my conscience. I am only doing my job.

All these thoughts are racing through my mind as I pull up to CCA. As I entered the front door I am greeted by a familiar face, the guard on duty, Ted. One has to go through the metal detector and the security check before you are allowed in to visit your client. Ted says, "Good morning William. What are you doing out here today?"

Ted always addresses me by my full name, William. When I first met him a couple of years back, he made the mistake of addressing me as Bill. I don't know why, but it always irritated me for someone to cut my name short and address me as Bill. I told

Ted then, as I tell everyone who shortens my name, "My mother thought enough of me to call me William and I'd appreciate it if you would too."

Evidently, I said it with a glare in my eyes and a sternness in my voice that caught Ted off guard. I didn't really mean to do that it just happens sometimes when I'm pissed off. Either way, Ted has been extra friendly ever since. Not that he was intimidated by me, but somehow or another he respected my demeanor.

All that is going through my mind as I look at Ted and say, "I'm here to see John Lester. I guess you know who that is?" Ted said, "Hell everyone here knows who John Lester is." Then asked me, "Is he guilty?" Even though I have enough facts to reassure Ted that John Lester is guilty, I think better of it and reply, "That's what I'm here to find out."

I quickly get through security, make my way to the visitation room and sit down to wait for my new client, John Lester, to come out and talk to me.

CHAPTER 2

*J*ohn Lester sits in his cell on this warm February day. The only reason he knows it is a warm sunny day is because one of the guards told him so. He himself has not been outside since he was arrested two weeks ago.

John calculates what he is going to say to William Harris, his new attorney, when they meet today and how John will behave. This would be the first time the two of them would meet. That didn't matter though, John knows all about the attorney he is about to meet. Everyone in jail is talking about William Harris. This new attorney is different. William Harris won his first two murder cases. Even so, John was not going to hire an attorney just because of what the losers he is locked up with say. John checked William out - it wasn't hard to do. The two cases William received not guilty verdicts on were all over the local newspapers for weeks. William acquired a lot of news attention for those two cases.

It appeared that William Harris was either lucky or maybe, just maybe, really good. John didn't merely rely on what the papers and the losers he was locked up with had to say about this new hot-shot attorney. He talked to Larry Hargrove about William Harris. Larry was not a friend. John didn't have friends or buddies. He didn't like anyone but himself. There were a few people out there that he let think he was their friend. He would pretend to be a friend to someone if it was to his advantage. He had a small group of fools that he let hang around him and let them think they were his buddies. These so-called friends were people that he could control. It gave him pleasure having control over some stupid fool who thought the two of them were buddies. That is what Larry is to John - a stupid fool he could control.

John had asked Larry to find out what he could about William Harris. When Larry came to see John, he told John that the word on the street was that William Harris was the real deal. There was even a rumor out there that William Harris had beaten a murder rap himself.

The next step was getting his adoptive mother to come up with the money and hire this new hot-shot attorney. Convincing his mother, Ann Lester, to hire William Harris had not been difficult; John was always able to get out of her just about anything he wanted. He had been fooling her since she brought him home when he was six years old. He knew, even at that young age, that he would have to convince this woman that he loved her. He would have to do that if he was ever going to get out of the foster-homes he'd been in. He fooled his mother into believing that he really loved her. He cried hard and clung to his new mother and she had taken him home to live with her husband and their daughter, his new sister. John would have been living there still if it had not been for his sister, Dorothy Lester. Dorothy cut a deal with John several years ago that was too good to turn down, so he moved out.

The only trouble with getting his mother to hire William Harris was Dorothy. Dorothy always saw through John. Shortly after he arrived in the home, if Dorothy had her way, John would have been cut off from their mother totally. He would have gotten the money out of his mother sooner if Dorothy had not gotten involved.

John hated his mother and his sister. As a matter of fact, they are both on his list. Either way he finally convinced his mother to hire William Harris no matter what the cost.

One thing is for sure - John knows how he will act when he meets William Harris. John will use his overpowering size to intimidate the lawyer. He is big, not necessarily muscular, just big.

At six feet-three inches tall, John weighs two hundred seventy-five pounds. He looks like an offensive lineman on a college football team. John is fond of standing close to someone he is talking to with an angry look on his face while staring intensely into their eyes. He does this even if there was no hint of trouble. John does this for several reasons; one - it scares almost everybody; two – it is easier to control someone if that person is nervous and intimidated, and; three – it gives him pleasure. It is important to John that William realizes that John is the boss right off the bat. Therefore, he definitely plans to intimidate and overpower William Harris at this first meeting.

John knows he is too smart to be in a cell waiting to see an attorney. John knew if he thought everything out, he could calculate how to kill a young girl and get away with it. He was right. John had taken the time and effort to make sure he did not get caught. He just wanted to kill. He did not want to get caught. If it wasn't for one silly mistake, John wouldn't be in this cell at all. That stupid mistake was letting one piece of evidence get out of his control that could connect him to this murder. But he isn't too worried. He is confident he has taken care of that mistake. Even though he is sitting in jail for killing three children, he is sure he will never be convicted of killing anyone. He is sure of this because he is smart and he knows the law.

The murder of ten-year-old Rebecca Springer, the last slut he killed, had been carefully planned out. Much more planning went into Rebecca's murder than the two previous murders. John's first murder was eight-year-old Tammy Mars. His second murder was twelve-year-old Patsy Oakley. John killed and mutilated all three little girls in the last sixteen months.

These gruesome killings were headlines in Nashville and across the nation before he was arrested. Although the story died down nationally in the months before John's arrest, there was hardly a day that went by that the local newspaper did not run a story on the murders. There were articles on what the murderer might look like. There was speculation on whether the murderer lived in Nashville or not. There was even a retired

Michie Gibson

FBI agent who did a profile of the suspected murderer. The profile was all wrong and greatly amused John. It gave John pleasure to read in the media the accounts of his murders knowing
that the police were nowhere near catching him until this last
murder.

The next thing John contemplates while he is waiting for
William to come visit him is how much of the "truth" John will
tell William. He will tell William all the gruesome details of
the three murders. He will also tell William how much he enjoyed killing those three bitches. he is not afraid to tell William
about these murders. John knows the law - he knows that William will be his attorney. He knows that as his attorney William
will never be able to tell anyone what he tells William about a
crime he committed in the past. John won't tell William about
his secret place or his "list". He will tell William that there is an
ironclad way that no DNA evidence will be introduced in court
against him. Even though he made a dumb mistake, he is sure
that he has taken care of it. After all, he isn't stupid.

These thoughts are going through John Lester's mind
when the guard comes and tells him that he has a visitor.

CHAPTER 3

I'm sitting in the large empty visitation room at CCA. It is a cold and uncaring room with grayish-green colored institutional paint on the walls. I'm preparing myself on what to say when the guards bring John Lester in to meet with me. The room is for the families of prisoners or approved visitors. The inmates housed at CCA are either awaiting trial or serving a short sentence. It is the same room where I met with my attorney to discuss my murder charge six years ago.

Today is not a family visitation day. I am the only one in a room that is about 20 feet by 30 feet with six tables for inmates to visit with family and friends. Attorneys are allowed to visit an inmate almost any time.

I've decided to play it cool with John when we meet. I'll let him know that I will work hard and sincerely to try and prevent the government from executing him. By taking John's case, that is now my job. I know that if John is found guilty, the government is going to try and kill this monster. I can't help but think that if John Lester is responsible for these little girls' murders. He deserves to die.

But it always comes back to the oath I took when I became an attorney. That oath demands that I work hard and do my best to save John's life. If John is guilty and I do manage to pull it off and prevent the government from killing him, that is ok with me too. The system will still be working. The system allows for a monster to hire a good and competent attorney to save his ass if possible. I have no problem with being a good and competent attorney even if it means that this miserable child killer's life will be spared. I don't have to like John Lester; I simply have to do my job.

I'm going to explain to John what I learned about his case from the investigators who work for the Public Defender's office. Those investigators worked John's case before his mother hired me. Laura Kincaid is the top attorney for the Public Defender's Office and, in my opinion, one of the best criminal defense attorneys in Nashville. Laura's investigators were thorough and she told me that the government has solid evidence which links John to all three murders.

In my mind, I feel that the most important thing to do with this meeting is explain to John what his options are under the law. I need to tell John that I think there is rock solid evidence against him and it might be in his best interest to allow me to work out a deal that will possibly save his life. John needs to know that any deal we might strike with the government to avoid his execution would mean that he will, more than likely, spend the rest of his life in prison. John also needs to know that if I am not able to strike a deal to save his life, we will go to trial. I feel like I have to discuss with him that if we do go to trial, my job will be to convince the jury that John isn't guilty of the murders. If I fail in doing that, then my job is going to be to try to convince the jury to spare John's life.

I'm positive that I won't lose any sleep if John rots to death in prison or is executed if he is, in fact, guilty.

I need to explain to John that the panties Detective Fowler found at his house have DNA linking him to the murder of Rebecca Springer. Because the murders of the other two children and Rebecca Springer's murder are so similar and gruesome in nature, the government might be able to convince a jury that John is guilty of murdering all three children.

It is important that I control my first meeting with John as I do with all my criminal clients. By control, what I mean is that I find it necessary that all my clients, including John, know the reality of what they are charged with. That means, I will direct how to handle the case. It also means that if I tell him the government has enough evidence to convict him, then that is the reality of the situation. Unless there is a way to prove the government's case unreliable or prevent the government from using the evidence it has, he will probably be convicted. I know from my own experience with the criminal justice system that everyone charged with a criminal offense has to accept the reality of what they are facing. What John needs to know is, unless I can find a legal way to keep Rebecca Springers' panties from being used by the state as evidence against him, this case is looking bad for him.

Still, I will handle John's case by the book. I've read the American Bar Association's Guidelines and know the Tennessee Supreme Court's guidelines and requirements for attorneys handling a death penalty case. I have the required experience and have attended educational seminars dealing with death penalty issues. I know I am qualified to handle this case. Most of all I have no problem earning good money for what I am about to do.

These are the thoughts going through my head as I doodle on my notebook paper when I am startled by a loud noise coming from the iron door that separates the inmates from the visitation area. When the door suddenly opens, John Lester is strutting through the door with a look of mayhem in his eyes. John is glaring at me as he quickly crosses the fifteen feet that separate the two of us.

I've seen the look that is in John's eyes from other yahoos in my life many times before. It is the look I got, sometimes, when I was working at Sherry's or in a club after I quit Sherry's. Every now and then someone would want to intimidate me just to let me know they were a real badass by enforcing their will over mine. John caught me off guard today as I wasn't expecting it, especially in this type of situation. I have never let anyone ride me like that in my club security days and it is not going to work here. Besides, I know John isn't trying to start a fight, he is only trying to let me know he is in control.

This fool is about to learn a new reality when it comes to

me. I sit and wait calmly while John rapidly closes the distance between the two of us. I don't move a muscle until he is no more than one foot from me and then I stand up abruptly, breaking his stride and making him stumble. Stopping abruptly has left John off balance. Before he has time to recover, I am on my feet and staring him in the eyes. We are only inches apart. I can smell it on John that I have terrified him.

I know I've caught him off guard and there will be no problem. Besides, the guards will never let it get out of hand.

I look in his eyes and ask him in a stern voice, "We got a problem?"

CHAPTER 4

*J*ohn hears William's question, which is asked in a tone of voice that means business. William's cold blue eyes stare into John's without blinking. John is furious with himself. He didn't expect the reaction he's gotten from William.

John fully expected to intimidate this attorney like he intimidated Laura Kincaid. John discovered in his life that people are easier to control if they are intimidated by him. But that didn't worry him right now, John knew he would eventually get control back over William.

First, John needs to get over how terrified it made him feel when William jumped up and got in his face. It made him think of what he feared most in life and that is death. John can sense that this attorney would just as soon kill him as look at him. John is used to hanging out at the biker bar and there are frightening individuals there. Those guys don't scare John as much as this attorney. John knows not to fuck with the bikers and he now realizes that William Harris isn't to be fucked with either.

After John has cleared his head and come to his senses, he is able to start thinking again. He realizes that this hot-shot attorney isn't going to kill him. Not unless he has to.

After John gets the fear of death out of his head, John starts thinking quickly as he always does when in a tight situation. John softened his expression and says, "Sorry, I've been in a bad mood ever since I got arrested for a crime for which they should never have caught me. I wasn't trying to start anything. Hope you believe me?"

CHAPTER 5

I know John is lying. John had meant to buffalo me. It didn't work out for him though. Nevertheless, that doesn't matter now. Now I know we can sit down and talk and I tell John in a low tone of voice, "Sure, no problem."

I start the meeting with the same no bullshit manner I do with every client I have represented since day one. John listens quietly while I tell him that I met with his mother and his sister yesterday, that his mother has hired me to represent him and that his case, due to what he is charged with, will undoubtedly be a death penalty case.

John's eyes glare and his face takes on a look of hatred when I tell him that I have spoken with Laura Kincaid. I tell him that the investigators who work for the Public Defender's Office gathered some evidence and information about his case. I let John know that Detective Randy Fowler, one of the homicide detectives assigned to his case, has found Rebecca Springer's panties at his house. The DNA on the panties proves that it was Rebecca's panties and that will make the government's case against him very difficult to defend.

After I got my preliminary speech over with and taking in mind that John has basically told me he isn't denying doing the murders, I realize he is only bitching about getting caught when he thinks he shouldn't have.

I look at John and ask him, "What's your side of the story?" I have never been more spooked by anything than I was by John's reply when he looks at me with a gleam in his eyes and a smirk on his face and says, "I killed all three girls and I enjoyed mutilating their young bodies and murdering them. " I'm sure the look on my face makes John aware that he is back in control of the meeting between the two of us now.

I find myself unable to speak or process what John just told me. After I listen to his confession, I sit there for a few minutes unable to respond. It comes to me that he probably wants to add something else but is too smart to say it. I am sure he is wishing he could tell me he will kill again.

I sit there and don't have anything to say. I'm sure I have a blank look on my face when John says, in a matter fact tone, "I'm going to walk on all three murders. That is if you do your job, counselor." It does not bother me that he is now insulting me by questioning whether or not I will do my job. The only thing I can think of is the way those three little girls were killed and this psychopath sitting in front of me is so giddy about being the one who killed them.

It makes me wonder if he really knows what he is talking about. I ask him, when I'm finally able to speak again, "Do you know how these girls were murdered?"

John laughs and says, "Of course I do, I killed the little whores! I kidnapped all three girls and took them to a special place of mine where I stripped them naked. I then tied them up good and tight so they couldn't move, spread eagled. Then I stuck a hawk billed knife in each one's pussy and pulled it all the way up to their throats. I looked each one of the little bitches in the eyes while they were dying and laughed. I even enjoyed the way they begged me for their lives and cried for mommy and daddy." Then he smiles broadly and says, "I'm going to walk on all three murders," he adds with a giggle as he shakes his head back and forth, "with your help that is."

After a long pause, I can only look at John in amazement and ask, "What makes you believe the government can't make its case?" He keeps grinning as he speaks, "Because there will be truthful evidence that shows that a man named Bobby Meyers brought Rebecca Springer's panties to my house."

My first question to John, now that my mind has digested

what he told me and I can ask a reasonable question that a lawyer should ask his client, is, "Who is Bobby Meyers?"

John's face tightens up as he looks at me and he softly speaks, this time without smiling or giggling as he talks, "Look counselor, I can tell you some of what I know but not everything. Let's just say I've broken some laws that you don't need to know about. I'm not worried about you knowing I've committed other crimes. It's in my best interest that you don't. I know you only have to sell me out when I tell you about a crime that I might plan in the future." Then he asked me, "Are we in agreement counselor?"

I take a moment to think about what he said. He is dead on about what information that I, as an attorney, can reveal that I obtain from a client. It is in his best interest not to tell me too much. Tennessee Supreme Court Rules of Professional Conduct mandate that I report when a client is about to commit a crime. Learning of a client's past crimes is privileged information. So, I look at him and say, "Yes."

Again, John's face breaks out in a big grin as he explains to me that Bobby Meyers is a low-life he met two years ago. He said that he let Bobby hang around just because he thought Bobby might be useful someday.

He tells me that he and Bobby Meyers have one thing in common, they both have a fetish for young girls' panties.

He then tells me that truthful evidence can be offered at trial that Bobby Meyers brought and left Rebecca Springer's panties at John's house.

I ask the obvious question, "Who would that be?"

John said, "He goes by the nickname of Wishbone. I don't know his given name. Wishbone is the leader of a motorcycle gang called the Outcasts."

I know about this particular gang. It is a local motorcycle club that has a reputation as a club that nobody wants trouble with. Tracking down Wishbone will not be an easy task. Finding Wishbone might not be the hard part. The hard part will most likely be whether or not I will be successful in getting Wishbone to agree to help, even if I do find him. I look at John and say, "Sounds like he might be hard to track down."

John quickly replies, "That's one of the reasons I hired you counselor. You're known as a badass as well as a good attorney. It is going to take both of those traits to pull this off and get Wishbone to testify. That's your job. Do we agree on that counselor?"

Again, he is right. My job is to find Wishbone and get him to testify truthfully. I reply, "Yes".

"Great," John says and adds, "you will also have to visit my flunky, Larry Hargrove. Larry will provide truthful testimony that will make sure that I walk on all three murders." I ask, "Who is Larry Hargrove and what will he say?"

John speaks in more of a monotone voice now as he answers my question. He seems to be more interested in getting the facts I need to defend his case than freaking me out with his unashamed and gleeful confession to murdering these little girls. In a dry voice he explains, "Larry Hargrove is a homeless man I met when he was living on the streets four years ago and I decided to put him to good use. At first Larry moved into my house and lived with me until I could make sure he was the right person for what I needed."

I am hesitant to ask, not sure if I want to know the answer, but I feel like it is my job to know what he needed Larry Hargrove for. John replied, "Larry was just what I was looking for. I didn't need a druggie but a total simpleton. I needed someone who was down on their luck and felt there was no way things could get better for them. Larry fit the bill. About sixty-five years old, Larry once had a family and a good job and then lost it all. His wife and children were killed in a car wreck. By making Larry feel like I was his savior and really cared about him most of the time, he became my stooge. I gave him a place to live that made him easy to control and he would do my every bidding. He would clean my house, do errands for me or just drive me to the bars and pick me up when I was ready to leave. I didn't want to get a DUI. Hell, I even paid him $750.00 a week so he could get his own place and car. I made sure he was totally dependent on me for his new life."

"That's fine," I reply, "but what will Larry Hargrove truthfully testify to that will help you?"

John replies, "Larry was at my house the night before Detective Fowler found Rebecca Springer's panties at my house. Larry will testify that he cleans my house and he did not see any panties in my house that day or any day for that matter. Also, Larry left my house that night driving my Mercedes with me in it. Larry will give truthful testimony that he let me off at a night club and drove my Mercedes home and that when he returned later, the panties were lying on my couch. That's where Detective Fowler found the panties when he did the "knock and talk" at my house the next morning. Larry will also testify that I had smacked Bobby Meyers around that night. Larry will also tell you that after I smacked him, Bobby got mad and told everyone there that he would get even with me someday."

John took a deep breath, looked at me with that shit-eating grin that he has had on his face through most of the interview and said, "Now I've given you everything you need to make sure I walk on these murders. I have provided you with factual proof that Rebecca's panties were in Bobby Meyers' possession. It can be proven, if his apartment is searched, that Bobby has a fetish for girls' panties. Bobby had a motive to set me up. Even a first-year law student should be able to prove I didn't murder those little whores. A hot-shot attorney, like you counselor, shouldn't have any problem at all. Bobby won't be found to say otherwise, that's all you need to know. Remember counselor, you and I agreed you don't need to know everything that I know to effectively represent me."

I know now that Bobby Meyers is dead and that John killed him. I have more questions to ask John. I want to know where he killed the girls, what he did with the panties of the other two girls he killed and what Wishbone was doing at his house the night before Detective Fowler found Rebecca Springer's panties. But most of all I just want to get the hell out of here. Those questions can wait. I simply say, "You're right." Then I leave.

CHAPTER 6

I leave CCA after my meeting with John Lester feeling like I have been shot at and missed and shit at and hit. I missed being shot when John thought he could intimidate me by bull rushing me as he came out to greet me. That didn't work for John. I knew my response had terrified John and that made me feel good. I could smell the fear on him. The rest of the meeting with John made me feel like he totally shit on me.

In my short career as an attorney, I have always been successful and take pride in my ability to handle a client. John is different. I have known my share of despicable human beings in my life, but I never thought I would sit in front of an individual who not only confessed to such gruesome crimes but was more than happy to tell me that he committed them.

The whole thing scared me. Not that John scared me personally. After listening to his confession, it would have given me some satisfaction to kick his ass. But when he was confessing his crimes to me, I felt helpless. I felt like I was at a horror movie and all I could do was watch.

Now I am second-guessing myself and wondering if I should have taken Laura's advice and skipped this case. I can withdraw as his attorney but the $100,000.00 is too big of a temptation to turn down.

All these thoughts are running through my head as I walk to my car and leave CCA. I left my cell phone in the car when I went into the jail. I need a minute to unwind so I sit in the driver's seat and check for any voicemail messages before I leave.

I have two messages. One from my legal assistant, Maria Lopez, the other is from Laura Kincaid, John's previous attorney. I will call Laura later.

Maria has been with me for about a year. She started working with me right after I opened my own office in Old Hickory. Old Hickory is another part of Metropolitan Nashville and the name comes from one of its founders, Andrew Jackson. Maria handles all of my divorce cases, preparing all of the paperwork and making sure I am prepared for court. I am more than lucky to have her working for me although most of the time I felt like I work for her.

Maria had four years of experience as a legal assistant when she started at my office. She knows how to handle the difficult clients that are going through divorces and make them feel better. That is one of the reasons I feel fortunate to get the large fee for representing John Lester. It gives me about a year's breathing room and makes sure that I can afford to keep paying her.

She is also my moral compass. We have developed a close relationship. She is twenty-five years old and her family is from Colombia. She speaks fluent Spanish, is about five foot six, has a slim build and has long black hair and dark eyes. She has a smile that I am addicted to. I can't help but being attracted to her, however, I keep everything businesslike except for some minor flirting between the two of us. I ignored Maria's advice when I took John Lester's case after she told me not to. When I asked her why she didn't want me to take the case, Maria said, "I can feel this man is evil and we'd be better off without him."

I call the office and Maria answers the phone. She lets me know that a couple of my divorce clients have called and she has taken care of them. She also reminds me that Dorothy Lester, John's sister, will be in my office within the next two hours.

Then, Maria asks me, "What's he like? He's evil, isn't he?" I give a one-word reply, "Yes." she responds in that tone of voice that lets me know she is not happy with me, "I told you not to take this case. You should drop it now before it's too late. You should fire him; you can do that. You know that." I answered, "Yes, but don't forget, we need the money."

Her reply, in the same disapproving tone of voice, is simple and reminds me that I am not always the one in charge, "We got by fine without him and we will if you drop him. Anyway, his sister will be here within two hours and I just wanted to remind you." Maria then said, "I'll see you at the office" and she hung up.

There is no way I would have forgotten my meeting with Dorothy Lester. She had been at her mother's side when I went to visit them in Belle Meade to discuss the case with John's mother. Dorothy hardly spoke at all during that meeting, but I got the feeling that she is the one really calling the shots. I also got the feeling that if she didn't approve of me, I wouldn't have gotten the retainer from her mother. I sure hope Dorothy isn't coming here to cancel the arrangement and take back the money, even though that might be for the best.

I remember every detail about my visit with John's mother and his sister yesterday in their Belle Meade home. Belle Meade is considered one of the wealthiest neighborhoods in Tennessee. It's west of downtown Nashville right next to Percy Warner Park. Although the park is nice and open to the public, it is more suitably located for the wealthy homes that border the park. The park has easy access to riding and wildlife trails. Real estate in Belle Meade is so expensive that even some of Nashville's biggest country music stars can't afford to live there.

When I pulled in, there were several news vehicles sitting in front of the house but they were not blocking the driveway. There was a guard at the gate who let me in after I told him I was there to meet Mrs. Lester and her daughter. I had never been in that neighborhood but I was certain that the neighbors were not used to that type of attention.

I was thinking as I made my way up to the house to meet with John's mother and sister that I had never imagined myself in this position when I became an attorney.

I have lived in two totally different realities. I have a life now and know people as an attorney that are completely different than when I worked in clubs. Being there, in that mansion in one of the wealthiest neighborhoods in the state of Tennessee, made me think how much my life had transformed in six short years.

I met with Mrs. Lester and her daughter in the study of the mansion. It was filled with dark wood and expensive leather furniture. Mrs. Lester was really nice and polite. She let me know that I must be a good man and a good attorney. Mrs. Lester said that she knew this because John had insisted that she hire me and John was a good boy and son. Mrs. Lester said that she felt that I was the perfect person to prove John's innocent of these terrible crimes.

What Mrs. Lester wanted most of all was for me to promise that John would never be executed. She didn't believe she could go on living if that ever happened. I told her that I couldn't promise anything but I would do everything possible to keep her son alive. I believed that when I met with John's mother and I still believe that now, although I have mixed feelings after meeting with her sadistic son.

Mrs. Lester told me that she adopted John when he was six years old. That in the foster homes where he had been placed, John had been mistreated. Mrs. Lester let me know that she and John had immediately fallen in love with each other and she needed him as much as he needed her. Dorothy didn't say a word while her mother was talking about John in that kind and motherly tone, she had a look on her face like she was not buying it.

I left John's mother and sister's house feeling really good about myself. I had a check for $100,000.00 for my fee and another one for $25,000.00 to be placed in my Trust Account for expenses. That was more money than I ever had legally in my life. Yesterday I had been feeling pretty good about myself, today not so much.

CHAPTER 7

*A*s I pull into the parking lot of my office in Old Hickory, I put the questionable thoughts about John Lester out of my mind.

My office isn't much. It sits in the middle of a strip mall with other small businesses on each side of it. There is a small waiting area for clients out front by the desk where Maria sits with photos of her family prominently displayed. My office is across from Maria's desk and I can look out and see her but my clients waiting in the outer room cannot see me. There is a larger room in the back. The room in back is where Maria and I work when she is getting me ready for a trial or where we eat lunch.

I quickly enter the front door to the office, nod at Maria and scoot my way back to my office. Maria barely acknowledges my presence and looks at me the way she does when I have done something that doesn't please her. Her disapproval of me will pass, hopefully soon. It always does, no matter what differences we might have. Maria always puts her full effort into making sure I am a good and competent attorney.

Once I get to my desk, I immediately become immersed in my files. I am returning phone calls for divorce clients and doing paperwork. Time speeds by and before I know it Maria is buzzing me to let me know that Dorothy Lester is here. A sense of foreboding overtakes me as I leave my office to greet John's sister personally.

I cannot help but notice that Dorothy is a good-looking woman. She has long shoulder length brown hair. She may be a few years younger than me and is very attractive. She is dressed in a tight cream-colored cashmere sweater and a black business skirt that shows off her shapely figure. I can tell from the look on her face that she isn't pleased to be here. I'm sure she has never been in a law office as small as mine. People with Dorothy's kind of money usually do business with the large law firms. I don't normally entertain that kind of client. Anyway, she is here now. I sure hope she isn't here to take the money back.

Dorothy doesn't waste time once she sits down and looks at me with a disapproving stare and asks me, "Have you been to visit with John yet?" I respond, "Yes, just got back from seeing him a couple of hours ago." Dorothy doesn't mince words, "You know he's guilty then, don't you?" She asks me that with no emotion at all in her voice.

Dorothy's statement caught me by surprise. I expected her to grill me about my qualifications to determine whether or not I was qualified to represent her brother. Instead, she is indicating that she knows what kind of monster her brother is. I guess I should not have been surprised. No way she could have lived with John and not know that he is a sick monster. Still, I have to be a professional and simply say, "The Board of Professional Responsibility Rules of Ethics does not allow me to discuss what he talked to me about even though he's your brother."

Dorothy replies in a terse tone of voice, "It doesn't matter to me what he told you, I know he is guilty. What does matter to me is my mother. It would be in her best interest if John never gets out of prison. An even better result would be that he gets put to death. That would be in everyone's best interest."

For the second time that day I am speechless. I halfway expected her to be on the same page as her mother about John's guilt or innocence, not advocating for him to receive the death penalty. It strikes me that Dorothy Lester is not fooled by her brother and she knows what a horrible monster he is. That does not matter to me. The long and the short of it is that it is not my job to protect Dorothy's mother from John.

I consider my words carefully before I speak, "I appreciate

your concern about your mother but she hired me to help John be found not guilty, if possible. She tried to make me promise that he would not receive the death penalty. I can't make promises, but I've already made a commitment to myself that I will do all that I can to win his case. That's my job no matter how I feel about your brother."

Dorothy looks at me and says, "I've checked you out, William. You're a new attorney with a good record. I was just wondering if you have ever been interested in practicing another area of law when this case is over."

I think I may have an idea where this conversation is headed but curiosity gets the better of me and I ask, "What do you mean?"

Dorothy sits back, takes a deep breath and says, "I'll answer that but first I want to tell you about John and what he has done to my mother and family."

Dorothy went on, "Shortly after I was born, my late father and my mother learned that she was diagnosed with severe endometriosis and could no longer bear children. They loved me greatly although I know both of them would have preferred that I had been a boy. When I started high school, we as a family, decided to adopt a child. Being a progressive family, we thought that the best thing we could do was to adopt a child that was in the foster-care system and give that child all the advantages our great wealth could provide."

"My parents had always wanted a boy so that was the first thing that led us to John. We knew he was six years old and that both of his parents had died when he was two. His biological father shot and killed his mother and then shot himself in the head. The reports indicated that John was in the room during the murder-suicide of his biological parents. It was two days before anyone called the police and John was found crawling around on the floor. There were no relatives to take him in so he became a ward of the state. John bounced around from foster home to foster home up until my mother and father adopted him. John and my mother became really close. He played to her desire to have a son and made her believe he loved her more than anything and that they needed each other more than anyone else. It became obvious to my father and me that John had fooled us at first into believing he truly loved us. But it didn't matter what we knew. My mother was completely under John's spell. No matter what he did she would never believe he was at fault."

"John is very smart. He was always a straight A student without studying. He knew how to manipulate our mother and always get what he wanted from her. She insisted that Father include him in their Will. Father agreed but made sure that it was set up as an Irrevocable Trust so John couldn't convince Mother to modify the Will after he passed. My father knew that if anything happened to him, John would waste no time in convincing mother to cut me out of her Will and make himself the sole beneficiary. Father made sure that I was the administrator of the trust and that I would handle the family's business affairs until my mother died. When she passes, John and I will be entitled to one half each of my parents' estate which is worth billions."

"My father died unexpectedly about a year after I finished college. When he died, I took over the family holdings and have been running the family businesses to this day. Even though I already had my own place by the time my father passed, I moved back home to protect my mother from John. I have been at my mother's home ever since then."

"John's cruel nature became apparent to me when John was about eight years old. I caught him in the back yard brutally kicking my sweet Cocker Spaniel, Angel, while she was lying on the ground. I grabbed John by the back of his neck and marched him straight to my mother and told her what he had done. When confronted by Mother, John ran to her and started hugging her neck and crying, saying that Angel was trying to bite him. I pointed out to Mother that Angel had been my dog for twelve years and the whole time she lived with us she never tried to bite anyone. My mother knew that John would not lie to her. My mother told John and I that we would have to watch Angel closer. When Mother said that, John looked at me and smiled that evil smile. The next day, Angel was found dead with her head bashed in lying by the road in front of our house. It is possible that Angel got ran over by a car, but I knew that John had killed her and there was no way I could prove it. As we were burying Angel in the back yard, John was looking at me smiling, knowing that I knew and I couldn't do anything about it. After that, pets in the neighborhood started to disappear or were found tortured to death. I always knew that John was responsible, but again I could not prove it."

"When John was about twelve, we had to take John out of school because he was becoming violent. At that time, John was much bigger than the other students. The headmaster told us that if John stayed in school, several of the other parents were going to take their children to another private school. From then on, we home-schooled John with private tutors. Even the tutors became frightened of him and we barely got him out of school and graduated before it became impossible to find another tutor to take on the job."

"By the time John was eighteen, the situation was getting worse at our home. He was constantly bringing people to the house that didn't need to be there and quite frankly scared the rest of the neighborhood. No matter what he did or said my mother always believed him which left me with no control over John. The only thing I did control was the money. My father placed me in control of the finances knowing that John was going to be trouble. That meant John couldn't get a penny unless I approved of it. He could always circumvent this by going to Mother and either begging her out of money or stealing it. Either way he got money but not as much as he wanted."

"I had to get him out of the house and away from Mother so I offered John a deal. I would buy him a house on the other side of town and give him $5,000 a week if he would stay away from my mother. Also, I told him I would buy him a brand-new Mercedes-Benz every two years. This was too good of a deal for

John and shortly thereafter, he moved out. Before he left, he told me that it didn't matter, Mother was going to die soon and he would own half of everything I've got right now. And he's right; when Mother passes away John will have access to more than one billion dollars. I hate to imagine what a man that evil and that smart with that much money could do. It scares the hell out of me." Dorothy told her story with a genuine somberness that made me realize that she was a good person who cared about people no matter what or how much money she had.

CHAPTER 8

*W*hen Dorothy is done talking, I thank her for the history on John. I tell her that it is going to be useful. But then my curiosity gets the better of me and I ask her, "What did you mean when you asked me what I was going to do after this case is over?"

She smiles and says, "My family has business holdings all over the world in real estate and manufacturing. I need a good negotiator and someone who's competent to handle legal matters for me. It would mean traveling the world and meeting interesting people. It would also mean that you'd be making $450 an hour with a $250,000 signing bonus." I know what Dorothy was getting at. She wants me to throw the case and make sure that John is either executed or never released from prison. I am thinking what a great offer this is and I would be tempted to take it if it wasn't for that damn oath I took when I became an attorney.

I reply, "No, there's no way I could do that."

Dorothy looks at me and says, "Why not? You could even keep your legal assistant. I can see that you're really attached to her."

I reply, "It doesn't look right. My job is to help your brother in any way I can. I hope you understand that." I also want her to know that's not the way I feel so I say, "I have to do what I have to do. It's a matter of honor and it's out of my control. I have to honor my oath to the law. That's all I can say. I appreciate the job offer and under any other circumstances I would have jumped at it but I can't take it today. Thank you."

Dorothy is quiet for a minute and says, "Too bad. I'll see you at John's hearing next week. I understand it's only a preliminary hearing." I tell her that is correct. It is merely a formality in this case but the government has to put on evidence to prove that John might be guilty so the case can go on to the grand jury. With that, Dorothy leaves.

When Dorothy is gone, Maria and I talk about my meeting with Dorothy. Maria tells me that while I was out meeting with John, she spent some time talking to Dorothy on the phone. Maria likes her and is surprised because she knows her brother is such a monster. I tell Maria that I like Dorothy too and that she has offered me a job that would keep Maria working with me.

When I tell Maria that the job would have had us traveling all over the world negotiating legal contracts and handling Dorothy's many businesses' legal issues, Maria looks at me and says, "You turned it down, didn't you?" I reply, "Yes, I had to. I hope you understand." Maria shakes her head and says, "I understand but that doesn't mean that I think you're not a cabron." She speaks Spanish when she's pissed. I've had to look up words in the past and already know that cabron means "dumbass" since it's not the first time she's used it on me. Anyway, she told me, in a sarcastic tone of voice, "Don't forget to call Laura" and abruptly left the room. I could have sworn she might be jealous when she was talking about Laura but surely not.

I call Laura and she asks me if I met with John that day and I tell her yes. Laura then asks me if I want to talk about it and if I would like to come over to her house later that night. I ponder my reply and say, "Yes, as soon as I get done working out."

CHAPTER 9

*J*ohn Lester is sitting in his cell feeling good about his meeting with William. He feels like he controlled the meeting.

John even manages to take control of the losers he is locked up with. It isn't hard for him to do. He can and does use his imposing size to bully the scumbags he is in jail with. He is also careful to make allies. He uses the sharing of his commissary, which he has a lot of, thanks to the deal he made with his sister. He also uses his superior intelligence to make some fool or fools think they are best friends.

The only part of the meeting John had with William that didn't go the way he planned was how William terrified him initially. It never crossed his mind that William would react the way he did when John tried to bull rush him. John was used to controlling people with intimidation.

John thought his attorney would not be expecting him to rush out like he was going to beat him to death. The look in William's eyes warned John that William would have killed him right then if necessary.

Death is what John fears most. The thought of closing his eyes and never opening them again is morbid and terrifying enough. But even more than death, what terrifies him is what comes after death. But John is certain that if this hot-shot attorney handles his case right, he won't have to think about death for a long time.

Besides, John had come up with an idea of providing credible evidence to his attorney that Bobby Meyers would be a good suspect for the one who killed the three girls. Even an incompetent attorney should be able to win this case.

John knew that when he described the gruesome details of the murders of the three girls to William, that the attorney wouldn't be so cocky. And it had worked. John had seen the look in the eyes of a defeated man after he told William how he murdered those girls and how much he liked it.

The problem was that he had made a mistake in his last killing. Kidnapping Rebecca Springer went okay. The girl's torture and murder at his home had gone just like he planned it.

John did his research and knew how to build a kill box. First, he built a wooden frame – using small light wood strips nailed together at the ends and able to stand by itself. The box was seven foot high. And it was eight-foot by eight-foot square. John used plastic sheeting to line the top, bottom and floor. It was easy to dispose of with no trace that the kill box had ever been in his garage after he killed the girls. John made sure that no blood or body fluids leaked out of the box and there would be none of the DNA from the little whores found in his garage or house that might connect him to the murders. John wore rubber gloves and thin plastic gowns from head to toe to prevent any of his DNA showing up on the bodies of the victims or on their clothes.

He knew how to clean up the scene after he killed the girls. He had taken all three of the kill boxes apart and thrown the parts in a dumpster. He made sure there was no excess tape, plastic sheeting or wooden strips left in his garage or house so there wouldn't be any suspicious items in his possession in the event his house was ever searched.

He had taken each of the girls' bodies that he tortured and killed to one of the rural counties surrounding Nashville. He disposed of the first body in Rutherford County, which is south of Nashville; the second one in Sumner County, which is north of Nashville; and, the last girl, Rebecca Springer, in Cheatham County just west of Nashville. For each body dump, he found a long straight rural road in a remote part of that county. He made sure there were no houses around and he would be able to see any cars coming from each direction. He would then back his car up to an open field and dump each girl's body along with her clothing, except for the panties. John liked to keep the panties. He liked to leave the girls' bodies stretched out spread eagle just like they were when he killed them. He wanted the parents of the girls to know how badly they had been tortured before he killed them.

Just knowing that the parents of the girls he killed were suffering gave John a smile on his face even though he was locked up.

He was careful not to touch anything, not even the girls' underwear, which he would keep as a trophy. He waited until he had taken the girls' panties to his secret place before he would touch them with his bare hands. Plenty of John's DNA was transferred to the girls' panties when he fantasized and relived the tortures and killings.

Finding a suitable location for his secret place proved to be difficult. He got lucky and found the perfect place. John rented a small isolated farm in Wilson County, a county due east of Nashville. He rented a cabin when he first started planning to kill little girls three years ago. The owner of the farm lived in California and was more than glad to collect the first year's rent in cash as a deposit and the money orders were mailed timely each month to pay the rent.

John was careful and made sure that it was almost impossible to discover that he was the tenant. Also, he knew if he kept a low profile nobody would ever be suspicious and try to find out who was renting the farm. He used a fake ID when he rented the farm. It didn't have running water and he never had the electricity turned on, so there was no record with any utility company.

The farm proved to be perfect. There are about twenty-five acres with no neighbors within miles. There is a long dirt driveway leading up to the old cabin where he kept his trophies in a back room. That's also where he killed Bobby Meyers.

The cabin is a small wooden house, about 50 years old, with two bedrooms and one bathroom, a living room and kitchen with a small eating area. He furnished it with cheap furniture from department stores and thrift stores. He didn't need nice things in his secret place. He set the second bedroom up as his Trophy room.

John made the decision that it was not necessary to tell William that he killed Bobby. In some ways John regretted that he did not tell his attorney about that murder. It would have been fun to see the look on the attorney's face when John described how he accomplished another slaying.

He got his point across and accomplished what he wanted to when he told William how he killed the little whores. He had controlled the conversation with William after that.

John first met Bobby Meyers at a strip club over on Eighth Avenue in Nashville about three years ago. John was a frequent visitor plus he figured it was a good place to find the kind of fall guy he might need in the future.

Bobby was also a frequent visitor at the strip club and John invited Bobby to his house after the club closed down one night.

Bobby was exactly what John was looking for in a patsy. Bobby wasn't a big man, standing at only about five feet six inches tall and skinny with black hair he kept greased back on his head. Bobby was the type of person John thought it would be easy to control.

John knew it was a bonus when Bobby told him that Bobby loved girls' panties and had a collection of girls' panties at his apartment. John didn't tell Bobby that he shared the same fetish.

The first time John became sexually excited by panties was when he was thirteen years old. He caught a glimpse of his sister, Dorothy's, panties. She was home from college for the summer. It was late at night and she had gone down to the kitchen in a t-shirt and underwear to get a glass of milk. He could

45

see her panties peeking out from the t-shirt, along with her long tan legs. He still gets excited thinking about his sister and her panties and what he'd love to do to her if he got the chance. That's why she's at the top of his "list".

Knowing that Bobby had a fetish for girls' panties made him a valuable person to keep around. John would use Bobby in the event he ever needed a chump to shift the blame to. Even back then, he knew Bobby would come in handy if John were to become a suspect for the murders that John was already planning to commit.

After John discovered Bobby was a panties freak, he slowly started making Bobby think they were friends. It started with John getting a couple of prostitutes from the strip club to come over and entertain the two of them at John's house. John would supply the drugs and the whores and he let Bobby become a frequent visitor to his home.

He hated spending the money on Bobby but it was a necessary expense. He wanted to cultivate Bobby as a fall guy in the future. Over time, John also couldn't help himself, and every now and then he would smack Bobby so Bobby would know who was boss and who was in control. He was careful not to overdo his mistreatment of Bobby because he might need Bobby in the future. He would slap Bobby across the top of his head from time to time. In fact, John had smacked Bobby around so much that he was always telling John, "I'll get even with you some day." John always knew that he was saying that to save face and he didn't mean it.

John learned some things from the first two little girls he killed and even from the last murder. He knew from then on, he wouldn't do any future killings in his garage. John would take the next little girl to his secret cabin. He would have to be careful and not drive out there too frequently in the meantime.

He also learned, after his second murder, that he needed a car that was not as noticeable as his blue Mercedes SUV in which to scout and kidnap victims. After reading the police reports that the investigators from the Public Defender's office provided to him, John learned that it was his blue Mercedes SUV that caught Detective Fowler's attention after he killed the first little girl, Tammy Mars.

He saw from the police reports that Detective Fowler learned that a blue Mercedes SUV might be the killer's car. Witnesses had seen his Mercedes more than once in the neighborhood of the second victim, Patsy Oakley. By chance, Detective Fowler spotted John in his blue Mercedes about a mile from where Patsy Oakley lived and followed John home.

John noticed right away that an unmarked police car was following him. He also saw the same unmarked police car parked in front of his house a few times after that with an undercover officer sitting inside. He now knew that the officer in the unmarked car was Detective Fowler. It didn't matter to him if Detective Fowler searched his house though, he knew that he had been careful and no matter how much and how hard his house was searched nothing would be found there to connect him to the murders of Tammy Mars or Patsy Oakley.

Still, John thought it was time to take a break before he kidnapped, tortured and killed another little girl. He gave it a little time and the unmarked car quit showing up in front of his house.

John took the necessary precautions before he killed his third victim, Rebecca Springer. He purchased a five-year-old white Ford Taurus with cash and never titled it in his name. In fact, it is still titled in the person's name he bought it from. That way, he could renew tags in the seller's name and there was no way anyone could trace the car back to him. After he bought the Taurus, he went to one of those storage places that people use to store their property near the mall and rented a stall for the Taurus under an assumed name. When he planned to use the Taurus, he would drive to the shopping mall and walk over to the storage unit. By taking these precautions, John's Mercedes would never be seen in the area where he rented the stall for the Taurus.

John only used the Taurus once and that was for scouting

and kidnapping Rebecca Springer. He was sure that no one had seen him snatch young Rebecca Springer. That is why John was taken by surprise when the same unmarked car with the same detective started showing up in front of his house a day after he tortured and killed Rebecca Springer.

Detective Fowler showing up at John's house wouldn't have been a problem if John hadn't gotten lazy. John always enjoyed disposing of the girls' bodies, along with the kill box, right after he killed them. He was careful never to touch anything with his bare hands and made sure he did not leave any of his DNA on their bodies. Tossing and leaving the girls' bodies in an open field made him feel good knowing that others would see his work and the parents of the young girls would be distressed about their "babies" being found in such a lonely place, naked for all the world to see.

The only reward John kept from the murders was each girl's panties. He would take the little whores' panties to his trophy room at the cabin in Wilson County. After he was finished with Rebecca Springer, he returned the Taurus to the rented stall in Nashville and walked back to the mall to get his Mercedes. Doing it that way made it almost impossible for anyone to follow him. John didn't see what could have made Detective Fowler start watching him again, except the fact that another little bitch was dead.

After torturing and killing Rebecca Springer, John didn't take her panties directly to his rented cabin in Wilson County. Killing the little bitch had tired him out and he decided, since he used the Taurus, there was no heat on him and it wouldn't hurt anything if he took the car back to the stall and waited a few days before he took her panties to the farm house.

He was surprised when the unmarked car appeared in front of his house so soon after he killed Rebecca. Detective Fowler showing up unexpectedly made him afraid that his house might get searched before he could get rid of Rebecca's panties. That's when John set his plan in motion to pin the murders on Bobby Meyers.

He thought it was too risky to flush Rebecca's panties down the toilet. He was afraid the panties could clog up the drain and it would bring too much attention to him if the toilet backed up and flooded. He had no place to burn the panties either. It was too chancy taking the panties in his blue Mercedes to get rid of them. He knew it was possible he might be stopped and searched if he was driving with the panties in the car.

With Detective Fowler lurking around his house, John thought it was a good time to put the heat on Bobby.

CHAPTER 10

With Detective Fowler's car cruising past his house, John knew it was time to set up Bobby Meyers for all three girls' murders. John figured the best way to do this was to have an independent witness testify that Bobby brought Rebecca's panties to John's house. That's where Wishbone fit into his plan to pin the murders on Bobby.

Wishbone is a leader of the motorcycle gang called The Outcasts. John got to know Wishbone from hanging out at a biker bar named the Devil's Hideout.

The Devil's Hideout is a tavern where he had enjoyed hanging out. John had plenty of money to spread around. He knew how to use his money to make people tolerate him even if he was never liked. He would pay the girls that hung out in the bar money to strip naked on the dance floor. That made him popular with the patrons. He got a thrill from the violence that was always present at Devil's Hideout.

He also set up a few deals with Wishbone and Bobby Meyers. John hooked those two up several times in the past for Bobby to sell guns that Bobby had stolen from somebody's home through Wishbone.

John knew that Bobby had a couple of pistols that he had recently stolen and needed to sell.

In the past, the way John set up the deals, Wishbone and Bobby would meet at John's house. Bobby would have the guns he wanted to sell and Wishbone would check the guns out. If the merchandise was in working order, Wishbone would send Bobby up to the Devil's Hideout with the guns to get the money for them. The bartender at Devil's Hideout, Tiffany, was the contact person for Bobby to meet with and get the money. Bobby would then come back to John's house and give Wishbone his split of the money for setting up the deal. Usually after the money was sorted out, the three of them would party with drugs and, occasionally, whores.

John's plan for Wishbone to witness Bobby leaving Rebecca's panties at his house worked. After Wishbone inspected and agreed to buy the guns from Bobby, Wishbone sent Bobby to Devil's Hideout so Bobby could get the money from Tiffany for the guns. John needed to get Rebecca's panties to Bobby, without Wishbone knowing it, and then convince Bobby to bring the panties back to his house while Wishbone was still there. John knew that he could not be there when Bobby brought Rebecca's panties to his house.

John had planned this all out in case the worst case scenario happened and the police found the panties before he could take them to his secret place. If his plan worked, it would be difficult, if not impossible, for the police to connect him to Rebecca's panties at trial.

John's plan was genius and even though he was locked up right now, it looked like it was going to work.

The hard part was getting the panties to Bobby after Bobby left the house to get the money for the guns from Tiffany. John knew that Bobby had a predilection for girl's panties and he was greedy and loved money. The greed and money were how he controlled Bobby. He needed to keep Bobby around so even when he couldn't help but smack Bobby, he would always tell Bobby he was sorry and give him a few bucks afterward. Not much money, but enough that Bobby would say, "It's all right."

On the night before Detective Fowler found Rebecca Springer's panties at his house, John gave Bobby a good smack in front of Wishbone because he knew how Bobby would react. Sure enough, Bobby said "I'll get even with you!" in front of Wishbone. Later, John followed Bobby out the door while Wishbone stayed inside the house. John gave Bobby Rebecca's panties, which were wrapped up in a plastic bag. John made sure his own DNA wouldn't be on the panties.

He told Bobby the panties were Tiffany's. John knew that Bobby had the hots for Tiffany and he counted on it. He couldn't blame Bobby for lusting after Tiffany, she was one fine woman. Tiffany was probably the hottest female in the bar. Of course, Tiffany wouldn't have anything to do with Bobby. After he handed the panties to Bobby, he suggested that Bobby might want to sniff and lick the crotch.

Bobby was only too happy to do that. He held the panties up to his nose and then licked the crotch like it was his favorite ice cream cone. That part of John's plan had worked, now the panties had Bobby's DNA on them.

The next part of his plan was to trick Bobby into bringing the panties back to his house while Wishbone was still there and after John had left. He did this by telling Bobby that he was trying to impress Wishbone and wanted him to think John was fucking Tiffany. John told Bobby that he had been bragging about fucking Tiffany to Wishbone and that Wishbone didn't believe him. He told Bobby he called Tiffany and told her he wanted her to send her panties back with Bobby when Bobby came to get the gun money. That way, when Bobby brought the panties back with him from the bar, John could prove to Wishbone that he was fucking Tiffany or she wouldn't have sent her panties to him.

John knew that this was a weak story, but he hadn't been worried. Bobby was too stupid even to figure out the panties were the wrong size or that the story made no sense. What was important to Bobby was money and sex.

Then John decided to make it more irresistible to Bobby, he gave Bobby five one hundred-dollar bills and told him he was sorry that he hit him earlier that night and wanted to make it up to him. John told Bobby that he would meet him later that night after Bobby left the panties at John's house. John also told Bobby that when they met, he would take him to a special place in the country where its business specialty was young girls. Bobby's face lit up when John told him this. Bobby was happy to be back in John's good graces.

After Bobby left to go to the bar with Rebecca's panties, John told Wishbone he was going to pick up some pot and he was going to have Larry drive him in John's Mercedes. He told Wishbone he could stay at his house until Bobby returned from the sale of the guns.

After Bobby left, he had Larry drive him to a local night club and told Larry that he would stay there and for Larry to drive the Mercedes home. John called a cab and had the cab driver let him out a couple of streets over from the storage unit where he kept the Ford Taurus and walked to the storage unit from there.

Bobby made all of this easy for John because he told John he was a sucker for young girls and especially their panties. Bobby bragged to John about his collection of panties that he kept at his apartment and had gotten at online sites where girls would sell their used panties.

He knew Bobby had to say exactly what he told him to say when Bobby left Rebecca's panties at his house. Bobby was to tell Wishbone that "these are for John." Although John felt like his plan for the most part was working, he couldn't be sure that Bobby had repeated what he told him to say. John would have to wait until his new attorney caught up with Wishbone to be certain what Bobby had said.

Bobby reassured John that he repeated exactly what John told him to say before John killed Bobby. John thought Bobby probably got it right, but he couldn't be sure until his hot-shot lawyer talked to Wishbone.

John smiled when he thought how he set Bobby up and killed him. After he got the Taurus from the rented stall, he called Bobby. He told Bobby he would meet him in front of the apartment where Bobby lived. John knew that there weren't any surveillance cameras at the apartment. He knew that surveillance cameras caught a lot of the stupid idiots that did not take into account that they might be on camera when they were in the process of a criminal act. John wasn't stupid.

It took an hour to drive to the farm after he picked Bobby up from the apartment. On the drive out to the farm, he found it incredibly difficult to listen to Bobby as he was driving. He was excited and in a good mood knowing he would kill Bobby before the night ended. Killing always filled him with great joy.

As he and Bobby pulled into the driveway that led to the cabin, Bobby became nervous about how remote it was and questioned him about it. He told Bobby not to worry about it that the owner had to keep a low profile because of the underage girls he kept for a few select clients. Bobby was so stupid he bought it. Bobby was still smiling when the two of them got out of the car. Bobby didn't notice that he walked behind him. He quickly looped a rope around Bobby's neck and strangled him to death.

Bobby's death had ended too soon for John. John wanted to kill Bobby slowly and make him suffer like the little girls did when John tortured and killed them. There wasn't enough time. Nevertheless, killing Bobby made John horny so he did take time to go into the cabin and pay tribute to the two pairs of panties and the photos he had of Tammy and Patsy in his Trophy room.

The trophy room was John's church. He spent his time there worshipping the souvenirs from his kills, the little whores' desecrated panties. John had envisioned filling it with items from future victims and surrounding himself with pleasant memories. Now that he's been arrested, he was going to have to move to a different killing ground and find a new place to worship his treasures.

He had already planned how to kill Bobby and get rid of the body before he left Nashville. The rented cabin was so remote he wasn't concerned with anyone catching him in the act. He didn't have time to dispose of Bobby's body right then, so he wrapped the body up in a plastic tarp and left it in a shed away from the cabin. Properly disposing of Bobby's body would have to wait. John wasn't worried about the smell when Bobby started to decompose because nobody ever visited the place.

Just thinking about killing Bobby reminded him what a thrill it was and how much he enjoyed killing living things. He first discovered his love for killing when he bashed his sister's dog's head in. That smelly dog, Angel, was Dorothy's great love. The dog slept with Dorothy and was hardly ever out of her sight. When Dorothy was visiting with one of her girlfriends, John lured Angel away with treats that Dorothy kept for the dog in the kitchen. He got Angel out to the road in front of their house and smashed her head with a big rock. He really enjoyed killing the dog. Not only did it give him great pleasure when he killed Angel because he knew how much his sister loved that dog, he also got an erection as he bashed its head in. He didn't realize what it meant at the time since he was only eight, but he knew now and he'd been getting that feeling as often as he could since then.

Killing Angel excited him so much that he started sneaking around the neighborhood enticing people's pets to come to him using treats. John would take the unlucky animals to Percy Warner Park, which borders the neighborhood he lived in, where he would torture the dogs or cats before killing them. Torturing and killing the animals always had the same results, it gave him great pleasure and he always got an erection. From the very first killing of his sister's dog to the last killing of Bobby Meyers, John knew that he would always kill when he had a chance. It gave him too much pleasure to quit.

Overall, even while sitting in jail, he was pleased with himself. He felt like his plan was working. Once he told his attorney that he planned on testifying that he knew nothing about these murders and all the evidence pointed to Bobby, his testimony would make sure that either the judge or the jury would cut him loose.

John knew that when he got on the stand and denied any knowledge of Rebecca Springer's panties being at his house, Wishbone's testimony would back him up. If his attorney did his job locating Wishbone and was able to get Wishbone to testify, that would prove that Bobby left Rebecca Springer's panties at his house without his knowledge. He couldn't wait to tell his attorney that when he testified it would all be over with.

CHAPTER 11

*I*t is colder as I leave the gym. It's a dark night moving in on what had been a warm day for February in Nashville. This day has kicked my ass. The day tired me out more than the workout at the gym I just finished.

This day started out with me being giddy as a schoolgirl. At first, I was on cloud nine for landing my first big fee. The money I received from John's mother is a game changer as far as getting my career started. Then the rest of the day had gone to shit.

I thought I could handle almost anything that was thrown at me in life but I never readied myself for a psychopath like John Lester. It is the first time that I've ever encountered someone who had no regard for human life nor cared that he had taken more than one life. The whole thing with John rattled me. After my meeting with him, I came to the realization that John might have figured out a way to beat his murder charges. I also realize that it is going to be my job to help John beat those charges.

Then my meeting with Dorothy had me questioning my oath as an attorney. It was clear she knew John is guilty. It was also clear that she wanted to make sure that he is executed or at least spends the rest of his life in prison. Dorothy wants to stop her brother from ever hurting her mother, another child, another person or animal again. If it wasn't for that damn oath that I took when I became an attorney, I would have jumped on her offer to handle legal affairs for her international business and let John be executed or spend the rest of his life in prison.

After all, making money is a major reason I became an attorney.

I had to turn Dorothy's offer down even though I want the money and I agree with what she is trying to do. I don't blame her for wanting John out of their lives. I found myself liking Dorothy and I think she is very attractive. Still, that was the right thig to do, I had to turn her offer down.

Now I am stuck representing a psychopath for a lot less money than Dorothy's job offer would have provided. A psychopath who I know needs killing and I can't do anything about it. I guess I can withdraw as John's attorney, but I don't want to give the fee his mother paid me back either. It doesn't help that Maria called me a dumbass for not taking Dorothy's offer.

Maria is on my mind as I head over to Laura's house. Maria and I have never had a romantic moment, but still, I feel myself being drawn to her. Lately, she has me wondering if she might be feeling the same. It surprised me that Maria might be jealous of Laura.

I don't know why, but I find myself thinking about my meeting with John again. I feel good about the reaction I got from him when he tried to bully me this morning. Seeing and smelling the fear that I evoked from John made me smile.

I can't say that John hadn't spooked me a little. Only a fool wouldn't be unsettled by him rushing out to get in their face like he did to me this morning. He is huge and looks menacing. I know that my reaction to him was a stupid move on my part. It would have been a mistake if he and I had actually gotten into a fight. I don't need to be in the news for fighting a client, especially one accused of being a serial killer.

I should have played it smart when John rushed out to meet me. After all, I knew he wasn't really going to assault me. We both knew that. I could have stayed in my seat, like any sane person would have done, and calmly talked to him. The problem is the only way I know how to react to a physical threat is meet it head on. It's just not in me to back down.

I am glad that I am going to Laura's house tonight and that I got my workout in. Physical fitness has been a part of my life ever since my early years in college when I was right out of high school. I was a walk-on for the college football team at Middle Tennessee State University. That was before I quit school and started working for Billy.

Even though I wasn't a successful college football player, being on the team taught me two things. One - I wasn't good enough to play as a starter on a college football team and, two - physical fitness is important. Even at 38 years old, I feel good about my physical fitness. At six feet-one inch and weighing in at 198 pounds, I am about the same size I was when I tried to play college football. Being physically fit always makes me feel confident in any confrontation I get into. I honestly believe that if it comes to violence, with just about anyone, I will find a way to prevail.

My mood is improving as I drive to Laura's house. I met Laura at a party a few weeks back. I knew her from seeing her around the courthouse, but had never really talked to her. At the party, we got to talking and she asked me if I wanted to go outside and smoke a joint. I followed her outside and she lit up a joint and I explained to her that I couldn't smoke pot anymore. When she asked why, I said because of the oath I took to obey the laws when I became an attorney. She then asked me, "Why did you follow me out then?" I replied, "To do this", as I leaned down and kissed her.

Laura and I didn't become lovers after we kissed at that party but we did start spending time together when we met up in court. So much so, people around the courthouse started talking about us as a couple. I like her, she is incredibly smart. She is also known as a bulldog for zealously defending the clients assigned to her.

On top of all that, she is really cute. I find myself at the ripe old age of thirty-eight having never been married, unlike most people my age. I haven't had a steady girlfriend since high school. The whole time I was going to college or working in the nightclubs, I didn't want to be tied down. I always wanted to keep myself free.

Now, as I get older, I sometimes find myself wanting a relationship, maybe even getting married and having children. Even so, with those thoughts in my mind, I am still not ready for a commitment. Although, if I do decide to settle down and have children, I feel like Laura would be a good partner or for that matter so would Maria.

There I go again thinking about Maria when I am going to see a beautiful woman that I think desires me. What a conflict. Maria and I have become close over the short period of time she's been working with me. She shares everything with me. I know her parents are illegal immigrants from Colombia. Maria was born and raised here in Tennessee. She loves children and cares about people. She even seems to care about me. Lately, she had started picking out the clothes that I buy. I don't mind. Although I am used to doing everything for myself, it seems natural to accept her help.

I caught myself thinking I shouldn't tell Maria that I was going to Laura's house. Maybe if it doesn't come up between the two of us, I won't say anything. Then again, I feel like I might be lying if I don't tell her. Damn Maria for putting these thoughts in my head.

I try to put any thoughts of Maria out of my mind as I pull into Laura's driveway and walk up and knock on the door.

Laura lives in East Nashville which is an older part of town where the millennials have taken to buying the older homes and either rebuilding or remodeling. East Nashville has become a trendy place to live. East Nashville is separated from downtown Nashville by the Cumberland River and is a great place to live if you work downtown.

Laura's home is a cozy red brick two-bedroom, two-bath house on about a quarter acre. It has a paved driveway and a fenced-in back yard. The street she lives on is wide and her house is at the end of the cul de sac.

Laura opens the door wearing a Tennessee Titans football jersey. I can smell the aroma of marijuana coming from inside the house as she lets me in. I can also tell she probably isn't wearing anything under the jersey. I can make out the outline of her breasts through the thin material. I know she is not wearing a bra. I would have bet you dimes to donuts that she doesn't have any panties on either.

After Laura invites me in, we go sit on the couch in the living room. She is sitting right next to me. She doesn't even bother asking me if I want to smoke a joint with her as she lights one up. I can't help but notice that the jersey has crept up past her thighs as she crossed her legs when she sat down.

She looks straight in my eyes and asked me, "How did it go today with John?" I let out a sigh, roll my eyes back and answer, "Not good, not good at all."

"What went wrong?" she asks. I pause before answering her. I can't forget that she warned me not to take John's case. I take a deep breath and then reply, "He is an evil son of a bitch and if I work hard and do my job, he just might have a case that can be successfully defended."

With a perplexed look on her face, she asks me, "How is that possible? The panties that Detective Fowler found at John's house have Rebecca Springer's DNA on them." I shake my head and reply, "I won't and can't get into what John said. You know that. Let's just say he has a chance and talk about something else."

Laura looks at me with an impish grin on her face. She is sitting so close to me you couldn't slide a piece of paper between the two of us and says, "Let's talk about your legal assistant Maria."

That question catches me by surprise, now I am perplexed. Why in the world would a woman sitting this close to me, who is almost naked, want to know anything about my legal assistant? I shake my head from side to side and sort of mumble, "Why do you want to know about Maria? She just works for me."

Laura leans back and speaks in a soft voice, "Surely you have figured out that I asked you to come over tonight with the intention that you and I will become lovers. After all, I know its

Friday night. I know you don't have court or need to go to the office tomorrow. And I know that you want to sleep with me. I even bought you a new toothbrush. I want you to know that I'm a one-man woman and I don't want to share you with anybody else. If Maria is competition, I want to know about it. It seems to me that she is more than just a legal assistant to you. I've heard the way you talk about her when we meet at lunch or talk on the phone. Also, I know when I talk to her on the phone, she seems more like your partner than somebody who works for you. I bet she even helps you pick out your clothes."

There Laura goes again, she not only surprises me with her thoughts about Maria, but how in the hell did she figure out that Maria started picking out what clothes I buy? It feels like I am getting my ass whipped for the second time today. Now I find myself in a position I'm not used to. I'm sitting next to a beautiful woman who's practically naked and don't have any idea what to do or say. Still, I always have to be truthful. With a long sigh, I look at Laura and say in a soft voice, "Maria is more than my Legal Assistant. I think about her romantically some-times but we have never kissed or even held hands. I also think about you a lot. I'm not sure if I'm ready to make a commit-ment. I haven't had a steady girlfriend since I was in high school. I've always wanted it that way, never wanted a commitment. I never had to lie. But I have to admit to you that as I get older, I've been thinking about stuff like that. Maybe not getting married right away, but at least making a commitment to try and have a life with someone. I'm just not sure if I'm ready to do that yet."

Laura smiles, leans in so close to me that I can feel her breasts pressing against my arm through the football jersey she is wearing and whispers, "I just wanted you to know I'm com-pletely naked under this jersey and if you want, you can spend the night?"

CHAPTER 12

*D*etective Randy Fowler is sitting at his desk located in the South Precinct of the Nashville Police Department staring at the computer screen. William Harris, the attorney representing John Lester, left a voicemail for Randy and he was trying to decide whether or not to call him back.

Randy is reviewing the multi-county task force file for the brutal murders of three little girls. These were the murders for which John Lester was charged and is now sitting in jail. For the last sixteen months there had hardly been a day when he hadn't scoured through the Department's digital files looking for a clue. The digital files contained all the information gathered by the detectives and officers working on the case looking for any lead that would help catch and convict the killer of the three girls. There were three detectives from Metro alone assigned to this case, not counting the officers from the other counties.

Even with all the detectives working on the case and all the resources allocated to the case, there were never any leads or clues that had panned out, not until Randy got lucky and found Rebecca Springer's panties at John Lester's house.

Randy was the only officer on the multi-county task force that followed up on John Lester as a possible suspect. Randy's commanding officer, Lieutenant Tim Harding, kept denying his request to allocate more manpower to investigate John Lester. Randy wanted to add John Lester as a person of interest for the murders of the three girls but Lieutenant Harding denied his request on several occasions.

In Randy's opinion, Lieutenant Harding shouldn't be in

charge of a Boy Scout troop, much less, be the lead detective on the task force the Mayor commissioned to catch the person who killed these three little girls.

Randy, like most everyone else on the police force, knows that Tim Harding has risen in the ranks by being connected through his family. Tim is not just incompetent; he is always looking to get his name in the news or be in front of the cameras.

Tim is good at two things; kissing ass and giving press conferences to the media. In his opinion that is a combination that nets few results.

In some way he really can't blame Lieutenant Harding for not adding John as a person of interest in these murders. Before he found Rebecca Springer's panties at John's house, there had been no hard evidence linking him to the murders. The fact that John drove a blue Mercedes SUV was not much of a clue.

The only common thread that Randy found during the course of his investigation was that two of the witnesses he interviewed mentioned that they thought they saw a blue Mercedes SUV cruising through the neighborhood a couple of days before the second murder.

At first, Randy hadn't considered that the witnesses who told him that they thought they had seen a blue Mercedes SUV were much of a lead. He figured there were probably a lot of blue Mercedes SUV's in Nashville and the chance that the killer would be driving such an expensive car was doubtful at best.

He wouldn't have spent time following up on that tip as a viable lead if it hadn't been for pure old luck. Two days after the second girl, Patsy Oakley, was murdered, Randy was driving back to the precinct after following up on a dead-end that Tim had him chasing. He just happened to pull up behind a blue Mercedes SUV stopped at a red light and decided to follow it on a wild hunch.

He thought it wasn't any more fruitless than chasing down the useless leads that his Lieutenant kept pushing on him.

When Randy ran the tags as he followed the Mercedes, he learned that the owner was John Lester. He had been following the blue Mercedes SUV for several miles, when it pulled in front of a house located in Donelson, a suburb of downtown Nashville.

The price range for homes in this part of town ranged from mostly middle class to some that were nice and quite expensive. John's house was in the latter category. The home sat on Knob Hill which consists of a small neighborhood of expensive homes that overlooked downtown. John's house had a driveway that ran about twenty-five yards to an attached garage. There were no trees in the front yard. Anyone looking out a window from the house could see not only downtown Nashville, but any cars passing by or any car sitting in front of the house.

When Detective Fowler first followed John Lester, he had a strong hunch that John could be the killer. That hunch was elevated to a gut feeling. As Randy watched John exit the blue Mercedes, he knew in his gut that this man was the killer that he and the task force were looking for.

It wasn't only that John was a very big man, it was the evil look on his face that gave him that gut feeling. He knew deep down that John Lester was the killer. Most people wouldn't think a gut feeling was enough to make this man a legit suspect for the murders, and they would be right. However, Randy's gut feelings had never proven him wrong in the past.

His gut feelings were so strong he was sure John was the killer the minute he laid his eyes on John Lester. He just had to prove it somehow.

Knowing that John was the killer was not enough to arrest him. He knew that he would have to make the case first. That's when he had gone to his commanding officer, Lieutenant Tim Harding, and asked to put more resources on John. Tim had looked at him and said in an exasperated tone of voice, "You are wasting my time."

After Tim turned down his request to investigate John Lester, he decided to do it on his own and keep an eye on him every now and then.

Ever since the second murder when little Patsy Oakley was killed, Randy would slip away when he got a chance to drive by John's house. He didn't care if John might get a glance at him. It might make John so nervous that he would make a mistake and Randy could nab him.

Randy continued driving by John's house for two or three months after Patsy Oakley's murder and would have kept driving by but there was only so much time he could sneak away from Tim and his watchful eye.

The morning after he got the call that Rebecca Springer's body had been found, he had driven by John's house to check on him and to see if he was there or might have made a mistake. Randy had John in the back of his mind as he drove out to Cheatham County where Rebecca's body was found.

Rebecca's body had been found in an open field, and like the other two counties that Tammy and Patsy were found in, Cheatham County is made up largely of isolated rural farm land. The killer had chosen his sites to drop the girls' bodies carefully. The only thing that changed was the counties in which the girls were found. The first child, Tammy Mars', body had been found in Rutherford County a bit south of Nashville and the second girl, Patsy Oakley's, body had been found in Sumner County which is north of Nashville. Rebecca's body, like the other two little girl's bodies, had been placed in an empty open field. The field was on a long road that allowed the killer to see a couple of hundred yards in each direction. That allowed the killer to drop the bodies off quickly and speed away without any chance of being seen.

Randy went to Cheatham County along with the other detectives on the task force to gather possible clues. Precisely like the other two murders, there had not been any clue or leads left by the killer at the crime scene or on the body. Also, like the other two murders, all of Rebecca's clothes, except for her panties, were stuffed in a paper bag lying next to her naked and mutilated body.

He spent the whole day where Rebecca's body was found

without anyone on the task force coming up with a clue or a lead. He knew that every piece of possible evidence would be sent back to the crime labs to be tested and analyzed for any evidence that would lead them to the identity of the killer.

He also suspected that, like the other two murders, the lab results would offer no clues.

He knew that it was necessary for the crime scene to be thoroughly investigated. Maybe the killer made a mistake and left a clue, you never know. But what he wanted to do was ride by John's house and check up on him. He knew that it was no use asking Tim for permission. So, he had to wait for Lieutenant Harding to close the crime scene later that night. Around ten o'clock, Lt. Harding sent everyone home for the night with instructions to meet at the precinct the following morning at ten a.m.

Before Randy went home from the crime scene, he took time to drive by John's house again. As he drove past the house, he noticed three cars sitting in the driveway. One was a ten-year-old red Ford that he had seen there before and had previously ran the tags which were registered to Larry Hargrove. The other cars were a red late model Chevy Camaro and a black Cadillac with damage to the right rear quarter-panel. Randy couldn't make out the tag numbers on either of those vehicles.

When he checked out Larry Hargrove, the owner of the red Ford, he found out that Hargrove had been homeless. It was the first time Randy saw the red Chevy Camaro in John's driveway. He decided to drive by the next morning before the task force met and see if he'd have a better chance of getting those tag numbers.

When Randy got up the next morning and rode by the house again, only the red Ford was sitting in the drive. The other three vehicles were gone. Randy decided to take a chance and go up to the door and knock.

He decided he would tell John that he was following up on a call that there had been a complaint of a noise disturbance at this address. It didn't matter to him that John knew that he was lying because he was sure John saw him driving by the house the day before. John had to know that he was under scrutiny. It was Randy's experience as a detective that a suspect would sometimes get nervous and make mistakes if the suspect thought he was being watched and had something to hide.

As he pulled into John's driveway and walked up to the door, he had two things on his mind. First, he knew he couldn't let Tim know about his visit to John's house. Second, he had to be prepared in case John decided to jump bad on him.

Randy had never been a fool. He knew that John would be a handful if he decided to get aggressive. That's why he had a stun gun in his coat pocket and if that didn't work, he made sure he could get to his Glock, if necessary. Normally, he would have taken another officer with him but technically he wasn't even supposed to be at his house. He hoped nothing happened and he could put some stress on John and nobody would find out he was ever there.

That's why he was somewhat surprised and relieved when Larry Hargrove answered the door. He was moderately relieved that he didn't have to face John and he was surprised when he looked through the door and saw a pair of panties sitting on the arm of a couch, in plain view, that you could have knocked him over with a feather. He knew right away who those panties belonged to - he just needed to figure out some way to get the panties out of there. After all, he didn't have a warrant and he wasn't even supposed to be there.

He had to think fast while standing at the door talking to Larry and looking at the panties. Randy first showed Larry his badge and asked him who lived there. Larry quickly let him know that John Lester owned the home but John wasn't there now.

He was quick on his feet and decided to tell Larry that he was following up on a complaint in the neighborhood that a neighbor had seen a man stealing underwear off their clothes line. He asked Larry whose panties were on the couch in the living room.

Larry blurted out that the panties were lying there on the arm of the couch when he got back to the house the night before, after dropping John off at a nightclub parking lot.

Randy knew he had shaken Larry up and he wanted to ask him where he dropped John off, but more than anything, he wanted to get out of there with those panties. He knew in his gut that if he could get the panties to a lab, he would bet his pension those panties were Rebecca Springer's. In fact, he might very well be betting his pension if Tim found out he was at John's house without permission and he was wrong about his suspicions.

Still, his gut feeling that John Lester was the killer was so strong that he had to take the chance. He was desperate to catch the killer of these three little girls and stop this from happening again. If he could stop the torture and murder of one more child, it would be worth his pension in his opinion.

He got his second surprise that morning when he casually asked Larry if he could take the panties to check and see if they belonged to the neighbors who had called in the complaint. Larry shrugged his shoulders and said, "Sure take them."

After leaving John's house, Randy arrived late to the task force meeting. He had Rebecca's panties in a plastic bag in his hand. He handed the bag to Tim and told him he was sure that these were Rebecca's panties and they needed to be sent to the lab to be analyzed as soon as possible.

When Lieutenant Harding asked Randy where he had gotten the panties, he didn't hold back. He told the Lieutenant that the panties came from John Lester's house and he was sure they were Rebecca's.

He could see that Tim was balking at getting the panties tested and lost his temper and started yelling at Tim, "If you won't test the damn panties, I'll take them to an independent lab and pay to have it done myself. When they come back as Rebecca's panties you can explain to the Mayor why you turned down a reasonable request from a veteran detective to test the panties."

The other two detectives in the room didn't say a word. They both knew Tim was full of shit. They also knew he could be trouble if you crossed him.

Lieutenant Harding took the bag from Randy, looked at him with a glare and said "I'll get the panties tested. You better hope for your sake that Rebecca's DNA shows up on them or you will be back on patrol doing third shift."

Lieutenant Harding was so sure that he finally had Randy and that the panties wouldn't have Rebecca's DNA on them, he fast tracked the panties to be tested. The Lieutenant was thinking that the sooner the panties got back from the lab, the sooner he could bust Randy Fowler and get him off his team.

Randy couldn't help but grin when the lab results were back and the results showed that the panties had Rebecca's DNA along with an unknown person's DNA on them. Lieutenant Harding didn't say a word to Randy when he announced the results to the task force and ordered the task force to arrest John Lester.

It wasn't just that Rebecca's panties were found at John's house that made Randy positive that he was guilty, it was the reaction Randy got when he arrested John. When he told John that he was under arrest for the murders of the little girls, John didn't say anything.

Randy had arrested dozens of people for murder in his career and had gotten a mix of reactions when he took them into custody. He found that most wanted to tell their story. That's usually what got them convicted. When he arrested John, he grinned big and looked at Randy with evil in his eyes and winked. That's when Randy knew he had the right man for the murders.

Still, Randy was nervous and anxious that he might not have all the evidence he needs to make sure John is convicted.

Lieutenant Harding gave a press conference immediately after the arrest. Of course, the Lieutenant didn't make a reference to Randy's contribution to bringing John in. The Lieutenant told the reporters that investigators were following his directions and used their intuition, due to the lack of clues in the case, and that is what led to John Lester's arrest.

Lieutenant Harding has no honor, which was the difference between Tim and William Harris, the attorney representing John.

Randy doesn't know William Harris that well, but he knows he is a man of honor. It didn't matter that the attorney had killed a man; he didn't care. William Harris had saved Randy's friend's life when he killed that man. He decided he would return William's call.

CHAPTER 13

*I*t's Saturday morning. I'm just waking up, haven't really opened my eyes yet. I don't have to look around to know where I am. I'm not where I thought I wanted to be. I thought I wanted to be at Laura's house in her bedroom lying beside her as we woke up and smiled at each other.

Instead, I'm waking up in my rented duplex in Donelson, the same Nashville suburb that John's house is in. I find it a little ironic that we live so close to each other.

The duplex where I live isn't much. The rent isn't high and that serves my purpose. Saving money on rent helps me keep my expenses down. That way I can afford Maria's salary.

For a woman that I'm not committed to, Maria sure does have a big impact on my life. If it wasn't for her, I would have woken up lying next to Laura. Maybe not, waking up next to Laura would still mean making a commitment and I don't know if I'm ready for that just yet.

I have more than likely blown my chance of ever waking up next to Laura. She didn't get angry when I told her that I wanted to stay the night but I couldn't lie, I could not make a commitment. She looked at me with bewilderment in her eyes and said in a soft voice. "Ok cowboy but if you keep this up, you're going to be riding fence posts by yourself the rest of your life."

I thought I knew what she meant when she said that to me. She thought if I didn't settle down, I was going to wind up alone.

When Laura called me a cowboy, it made me think about

how different my life is now than when I worked for Billy at Sherry's. In those days I fantasized that I was something like a cowboy or an outlaw living on the fringe. I knew what I was doing could lead to violence and maybe somebody getting hurt. The fact that somebody might get hurt didn't especially concern me. Everyone involved knew that, either working at Sherry's or selling pot out the backdoor, we were a little bit North of the law and had crossed the line. We all knew we could go to jail if we got caught. That's why we policed ourselves-. Thinking like that was what led to me picking up a murder charge.

CHAPTER 14

*W*hen I worked for Billy at Sherry's, I made extra money helping out Jack Adams. Jack was a loan shark who hung out at Sherry's. Working for Jack was what led to my arrest six years ago and me being put on trial for murder.

Jack had a wholesale marijuana business in addition to his loan shark business. He would buy about one hundred pounds of pot at a time from Mendocino County California. He usually paid around $1,000.00 per pound in cash. He would up the price to $2,000.00 and distribute it in ten to twenty pound lots to various dealers who worked for him. Those dealers would then up the price to $3,000.00 per pound and sell it to street level dealers who sold the pot in ounces for around $400.00 per ounce.

The deliveries came in about once a month from Jack's contact in California. He would pay me $5,000.00 to go with him and be security when he would have a pick up. I thought of this endeavor as a big adventure. Back in those days, I was living my life like it was a B grade movie. I never thought about the consequences of what I was doing just like I did everything else. I knew I didn't want to kill anybody but if someone tried to rip us off it was my job to take care of business.

I had accompanied Jack a couple of times before and nothing had gone wrong. But even so, I decided that this was my last gig with Jack. The money was great and Jack would give me and Dakota a good deal on the pot we bought from him. The fact was that neither Dakota nor I liked him.

I got to know Jack because he was one of the regular patrons who hung out at Sherry's. He let everyone know that he was a badass. Actually, he was never all that tough unless he had backup with him, which he always did. I heard him brag about how much he enjoyed watching his thugs mercilessly beat some poor slob who was late on their payments to Jack. It was rumored that he liked to smack the young girls around who were lured to him because of his money.

If it wasn't for the $5,000.00 he was paying me, I would not have had anything to do with him. Working for Jack was comparable to what I am doing with John Lester. If it wasn't for the $100,000.00 John's mother is paying me, I wouldn't have anything to do with that psychopath either.

I once asked Jack why he paid me so much money and didn't use one of his regular guys who handled his debt collections. he said, "Look, William I'm doing a deal with me carrying anywhere from $100,000.00 to $150,000.00 in cash. I need someone who can take care of me, my money and any situation that might come up. I've been in the club and have seen how you and Dakota handle yourselves. I feel like me and my money are safe with you along. That's what makes you worth it." Nevertheless, I let him know that I wouldn't be working for him in the future.

He told me he was ok with this being my last time as his security. He also let me know that this time he was dealing with a different guy bringing in the load that night. Because it was a new guy, He changed the drop to Bordeaux, a rural area a few miles east of Nashville. All the previous drops had been in one of his warehouses near downtown Nashville. Tonight, we were meeting at a deserted farmhouse with no neighbors close by. Didn't matter to me though. This was my last time doing these pickups with him. Still, it felt like an adventure.

Jack and I arrived at the farmhouse before the truck with the load of pot got there. When the truck pulled up, the driver got out. Jack asked me to walk up the driveway to the road that ran in front of the farmhouse while he finalized the deal with the driver. It took me about ten minutes to walk up the driveway and back. When I got back to where Jack and the driver were, it quickly became obvious to me that the deal had gone south. Jack had pulled a pistol on the driver. The driver had his hands above his head, with his back to the truck. Jack was standing about four feet from him while pointing the pistol at the driver's head. When I saw this, I slowly pulled my Glock and approached with caution.

As I walked up, Jack was standing in front of me facing the driver. At that time, I had no idea what was going on or why he was holding the driver at gun point. There was a pistol lying on the ground between the two of them. I had a sinking feeling in my head that this wasn't going to end well unless I could convince Jack to stand down. Even if the driver had tried to rob Jack and Jack had somehow got the drop on him, which had thwarted the robbery, there was no good reason to hurt the driver. I had to convince Jack to let it go.

I slowly walked up to Jack and asked him in a low voice, "What's going on?"

Jack never took his eyes or gun off the driver as he replied to my question, "This guy is a cop. His real name is Bob Lyons. He doesn't remember me, but he busted a buddy of mine for theft a couple of years back. I saw this pig in court when he testified against my friend but he didn't see me. When you were half way up the driveway, I finally figured out who he really is. I pulled my gun on him and waited for you to get here."

I was trying to take all of this in. At the same time, I was trying to come up with a way to end this situation without anyone getting hurt or Jack and I going to jail.

I looked over at the man being held at gunpoint and asked him, "Is it true? Is your name Lyons and are you a cop?"

Lyons looked straight at me with a look of defiance, and said with no hint of fear in his voice, "That's right. I'm a cop and the two of you should give yourselves up right now."

When I first discovered that the driver was a cop, I entertained a fleeting thought that maybe we could work out a deal. We let him go and he lets us go. I could tell by Officer Lyons' demeanor that idea was not going to work.

I remembered looking at Jack and telling him, "It's over. We're both caught. Drop your weapon, nobody is going to die over this." Jack had a crazy look in his eyes and yelled at me, "What the hell are you talking about?! We're not caught. This cop is caught! Nobody knows he's here. I've got lookouts posted up the road and they would have called my cell if someone was shadowing him. All I have to do is kill this fucker and we both walk free. What do you care anyway he's just a cop and why do you think I'm paying you $5,000.00?" My reply was short and to the point, "Doesn't matter who he is, no one is going to kill him. Not while I can stop it."

Jack turned his head away from Officer Lyons and was looking straight at me and yelling, "You can't stop me!" He then started to turn his head back towards Officer Lyons, I made a quick one-word reply, "Wrong," as I shot Jack in the side of his head before he could pull the trigger and kill Officer Lyons.

After I shot Jack, I walked over to Officer Lyons, who was still standing with his back against his truck. I handed him my Glock and said, "I guess this is where you arrest me."

Officer Lyons didn't say a word to me at first. He took my gun and used his cell phone to call for backup. When the backup got there, he walked over to me and said, "Thanks," right before I was handcuffed, put in the back of a patrol car and taken to jail.

CHAPTER 15

I spent my first night in jail, which wasn't my last, after Officer Lyons arrested me six years ago. For the next ten months, I went to sleep and woke up in jail. The whole time I was locked up, I knew I might spend the rest of my life in jail if I was found guilty of felony murder for killing Jack Adams.

Up until this arrest, I had never spent one night in jail. I never gave going to jail much thought when I was working for Billy at Sherry's or doing the various other things that could have easily landed me there. I always thought that if I got caught, I would be able to tough it out and do the time.

I was only half right. I was enough of a badass that I was able to do ten months locked up without too much trouble. I was only challenged once by another inmate during the time I was locked up. His nickname was Razor Blade. Blade as he liked to be called, like me, was in jail on a murder charge. He had been accused of slitting his wife's throat.

I met Blade on my first day in jail when we were eating lunch. I was standing in line, waiting my turn to be served my meal – or what they call a meal. The rock boys or servers would dole out the food onto the plates we were holding in our hands. As we passed by, a rock boy would slam the slop we were being fed onto our plates with oversized ladles.

Blade walked up to me while I was standing in line, shoved me out of line and took my place. I acted on instinct and slugged Blade in the jaw knocking him to the floor.

I spent the next thirty days in the hole for fighting. When I got out, I learned that I had broken Blade's jaw and that he was no longer in our local jail. He accepted a deal and pleaded guilty to murdering his wife. It didn't hurt my feelings when I found out Blade had been sent off to prison with his jaw wired shut.

After that, I did nine more months in jail and never had any more trouble.

From then on, I knew I had what it took to survive being locked up. That meant you had to be tough. Being tough wasn't the problem, time was the problem. I was wrong when I thought I could do the time. I learned my first day in the hole, with the loss of my freedom, that time was my biggest enemy. When I was locked up, time slowed down for me. So much so, that I avoided looking at a clock.

Dakota, with the help of Billy, raised the money and hired Marvin Jones to represent me for my felony murder charge. Marvin was and still is a top-notch attorney in Nashville and I found him to be a straight shooter.

I liked Marvin from the start. He came to visit me at least once a week while I was in jail after Dakota and Billy hired him. Since I've become an attorney, I've tried to pattern my law practice like Marvin's and treat my clients like he treated me.

I spent as much time as possible in the law library the jail provided. I researched, looking for anything that might prevent me from spending the rest of my life in prison. That research is how I came up with the idea of arguing "jury nullification" as my only hope of being found not guilty at trial. The research taught me the legal theory of jury nullification. This is a concept where members of a trial jury can find a defendant not guilty even if he is guilty. To find jury nullification, the jurors would have to be convinced that either: they should not support the government's law; they don't believe the law is constitutional or humane; or they don't support the punishment a defendant might receive for breaking that law. I was counting on the jury not supporting the punishment I might receive for killing Jack Adams. I was certain the jury would not want to punish me because I had saved the life of a respected Nashville police officer.

I spoke with Marvin about the possibility of arguing jury

nullification and he told me to forget about it. He felt that there was no way Judge Susan Hart, the judge assigned to my case, would allow us to argue jury nullification. Marvin told me that if he even tried to make that argument, the Judge would find him in contempt and possibly lock him up for his efforts. I listened to Marvin but still kept the idea in my mind.

I occupied the time in jail waiting for my trial by staying physically fit and continuing to study the law. In the Sheriff's Law Library, I tried to learn as much as I could about the laws and rules of evidence that would affect my case. It wasn't that I didn't trust my attorney, I wanted to know what was going on and what to expect. I talked to him about my research and would ask him questions. He always listened to me and would thoughtfully answer and explain any questions I might have.

I got into a routine waiting for my trial. I would go to the gym in the mornings and was able to get to the law library for about one or two hours in the afternoons. On Saturdays, Dakota never missed a chance to visit the entire time I was locked up.

It didn't matter how much I tried to occupy my time in jail, time remained my biggest enemy. No matter what I did, I would wake up every day with nothing to look forward to. I knew back then that if I was lucky enough to get out of jail it would be hard, if not impossible, for me to find any adventure that was worth taking a chance on landing me back there.

The nights and days dragged on waiting for trial. Still the time passed and my trial was one day away when my attorney came to see me for the last time.

Marvin explained to me that he had worked out a deal with the Assistant District Attorney, Lindsey Moreland. Ms. Moreland was prosecuting my felony murder case and was known and proven to be a tough prosecutor.

Marvin told me that the D.A. had agreed to reduce my felony murder charge to manslaughter, with six years to serve. I would be given credit for time already served.

I shook my head and said, "That's not a fair deal. I should get straight probation. I've done enough time for saving that cop's life." My idea that I should get probation was based on my heartfelt belief that justice would be served with me being placed on probation. I knew that I wasn't the only person that felt that way. I kept up with the media following my case. Although Officer Lyons never made a public statement regarding what he thought would be a good outcome to my case, the Chief of Police made a public statement that he and the department hoped the system would show me some leniency.

Marvin reached back and put his hands behind his head while looking in the air and said, "I agree with you and I tried as hard as I could to persuade Lindsey to agree to straight probation. There's absolutely no way she will change her mind."

Marvin leaned forward, sat up straight in his chair and looked me straight in the eyes and said in a no-nonsense tone of voice, "William it's a shitty deal, but I think you should take it. If the jury looks at the facts and follows the law you are more than likely going to be found guilty of felony murder. That means you will probably spend the rest of your life in prison. As fond as I am of you, it's my duty to tell you that I've been trying criminal cases for a long time and you can't win this trial."

That I would have to spend five more years locked up wasn't what I wanted to hear Marvin say. I weighed all the facts and I firmly believed that I was going to be offered probation from the government and would have been out of jail in a few days. That would have been a fair deal.

I vividly remember sitting in jail listening to Marvin advising me that I should agree to another five years in jail. The thought of staying in jail five more years was more than I could stomach. I decided to bet it all and take a chance that by the end of the week I would be free or on my way to prison for a long time, if not the rest of my life.

I looked at Marvin and said, "My trial can be won if the jury can be convinced to find me not guilty. Even though the facts and the law say I am guilty. Justice would be better served if I walked free. What I want to argue is jury nullification."

Marvin looked at me and shook his head and said, "I told

you that I can't argue jury nullification. Judge Hart would never give me permission to present that argument to the jury. I don't even want to ask her."

I replied, "Maybe the best thing to do is not ask Judge Hart for permission. Maybe you should let her hear it for the first time when the legal theory is put before the jury."

His eyes got wide and his tone grew stern and unwavering when he said, "I can't and I will not present to a jury the legal defense of jury nullification without requesting permission from the court. It would be unethical for me to do so. Let me repeat myself - I can not do it."

It only took me a split second to reply, "You won't have to. I'm going to do it. You're off the hook. I'm going to be my own attorney tomorrow at trial. You're fired. No hard feelings though. I really appreciate everything you've done for me."

Marvin used every argument he could think of in his efforts to persuade me to change my mind and let him continue to represent me. He told me how I was not prepared for the ins and outs of a jury trial. He tried to convince me that I would be at the mercy of Lindsey Moreland who is a seasoned and skillful prosecutor. He was emphatic that I would be found guilty. He let me know how hard it would be for me, as a lay person, to represent myself successfully.

Marvin told me that attorneys rarely represented themselves in court because attorneys knew it was a bad idea. He told me that it never worked out for the attorney who decided represent themselves. He said there was a saying in legal circles that an attorney who represented themselves had a fool for a client.

I guess he could tell he wasn't making any headway on getting me to change my mind. I was going to represent myself the next day no matter how hard he tried to talk me out of it. Finally, in desperation, he yelled at me, "What the hell do think tomorrow is going to be?!"

My answer to his question was accompanied by the first smile I had on my face in a long time and I said, "A big adventure.

Maybe the last one."

CHAPTER 16

*T*he next day it was a surprise to everyone when it was announced in court that I had fired Marvin and would be my own attorney. I told Judge Hart that Marvin was a good attorney, but I came to the conclusion that it was in my best interest to represent myself.

Judge Hart acted like she was reluctant to grant my request to be my own attorney. She even suggested that she thought I was doing this so I could get a continuance.

I gently reminded Judge Hart that the constitution guaranteed me the right to represent myself. I told her, "I don't need a continuance. I need a trial and I am ready today if you are." Judge Hart bristled and let me know in no uncertain terms she was not amused with my court manner when she stared at me and sternly said, "And a trial you shall have. But I can almost guarantee you that you won't like the results."

I listened to what the Judge said and shrugged my shoulders as I replied, "There are few guarantees in life. But the constitution does guarantee me a fair trial and I trust you will give me one."

The Judge's response was convincing, "I can guarantee you that."

The trial went quickly after the jury was chosen. Judge Hart kept her word and gave me a fair trial. She sustained some of my objections to questions that the D.A. asked the witnesses. The Judge would only sustain my objections if I cited the correct rule of evidence that the D.A. might be violating. The same went for me, if I was in violation of the rules of evidence when questioning a witness and the D.A. objected, Judge Hart would sustain her objection. As the trial went on, Judge Hart seemed to warm up to me. I think she appreciated that I knew what I was doing and acted professionally.

The climax of my trial came when Officer Lyons testified and the D.A. questioned him. He told the jury that he was a Nashville police officer who was working undercover as a drug dealer selling marijuana in a reverse sting operation. On the night in question, the officer made a deal with the deceased, Jack Adams, to sell one hundred pounds of marijuana to him. Officer Lyons stated that when he arrived at the agreed upon location for the deal to go down, Jack and I were already there waiting to purchase the marijuana. He told the jury that I left the two of them and walked up the driveway to the road to see if anyone had been following him. While I was gone, Jack recognized that he was a police officer and pulled a gun on him. Jack made him drop his weapon while pointing a gun at his head and making him back up to the truck that held the marijuana. He told the jury that that's when I walked back up, saw what was going on, and pulled a weapon. Officer Lyons testified that I told Jack to drop his gun that he wasn't going to kill anybody. He spoke with passion as he told the jury that Jack wouldn't drop his weapon and would have killed him if I hadn't shot and killed Jack. Then he turned his gaze away from the jury, looked straight at me and said, "Thank you, William."

After Officer Lyons' testimony, I felt certain that I had a chance if I could convince at least one juror that justice would be better served by letting me go home.

When it was my turn to cross-examine Officer Lyons, I only had one question for him. I knew that my one question was an inquiry that the D.A. would object to. I also knew Judge Hart would get pissed. That didn't matter to me though, I wanted the jurors to hear the question even if they didn't hear Officer Lyons' answer. I was sure that my question to Officer Lyons would beg the answer I needed the jurors to hear.

With that in mind, I stood up and walked to the podium,

Michie Gibson

took a deep breath, looked at Officer Lyons and asked him my one and only question, "Officer Lyons do you want the jury to convict me for the crimes I'm accused of committing here today?"

The D.A. quickly jumped up and loudly yelled, "Objection!", before Officer Lyons could answer my question. Judge Hart looked at me with a frown on her face and quickly barked, "sustained" to the D.A.'s objection.

Judge Hart then turned her attention to the jurors and told them to disregard my question and not let the question influence their decision making when determining my guilt or innocence. She told the jurors with a stern and unequivocal tone to her voice that, "This case will be decided on the facts and the law that applies to those facts." She then turned her attention back to me and proceeded to scold me in front of the jurors. "Mr. Harris you know better than to ask a question like that of a witness. Don't do it again." I said, "Yes ma'am. It won't happen again." Then I announced to the Court, "No more questions of this witness your honor", and sat down. I felt like I made my point.

Officer Lyons left the witness stand. It was then time for the attorneys to give their closing arguments to the jury. The D.A.'s argument was more than an hour long. She reminded the jurors that the facts of the case had proven beyond a reasonable doubt that I was committing a felony when I was with Jack Adams to purchase marijuana. She also said it was an undisputed fact that I had killed Jack Adams in the commission of that felony. She told the jurors, correctly, that the law didn't allow an exception for a killing that was committed to save an innocent man. She let the jurors know that she was grateful that I had saved Officer Lyons' life but that that didn't negate the fact that I was still guilty of felony murder.

I listened to the D.A.'s closing argument and knew she was right about the laws and the facts. I also knew that my closing argument would be much shorter than hers and that I would not get to finish my argument to the jurors. To top it off, I was sure my argument to the jurors would piss Judge Hart off again. But my life was at stake and I didn't give a damn how the Judge felt!

I stood in front of the podium when it was my turn to address the jurors. I took a deep breath and tried my best to make eye contact with each individual juror as I gazed out over the jury pool. I put my hands in my pockets as I spoke to the jurors. (Something I still do today when I'm making an argument whether it is before judge or a jury.) I spoke softly when I addressed the jurors, "Lindsey Moreland, the government's Assistant District Attorney, who is prosecuting me, shot straight with you. I am guilty as charged. Having said that, I hope you as the jury will agree with me, that sending me to prison under this set of facts would be an injustice and that a jury, with a conscious, should and can ignore the law. Find me not guilty and let me go home."

D.A. Moreland jumped to her feet quickly again and yelled at the top of her voice, "Objection!"

Judge Hart wasted no time sustaining the objection. The Judge turned to the jurors and told them to disregard my statement. Next, she turned to me, while making no effort to temper her anger, as she stared at me and said, "Mr. Harris I told you not to ask that question again." I looked at her and shrugged my shoulders. When I replied to her obvious anger over my argument to the jurors, I said to her, "I didn't ask a question. I was simply letting the jurors know what I think they should do."

My response seemed to anger Judge Hart even more. She glared at me and said with utter disdain in her voice, "Mr. Harris do not try this stunt again or I will find you in contempt of this Court for which you will go to jail." I looked at Judge Hart and said, "Ma'am I'm in jail right now. I just want to get out. That's why I did what I did. I hope you understand. But I have nothing more to say to the jury." I then sat down. I knew the Judge couldn't un-ring that bell. The jurors heard what I said and they would remember it when they went back to deliberate, no matter what Judge Hart told them not to consider.

When the jurors left the courtroom to decide my fate, I

felt confident at first that they would find me not guilty. I was counting on at least some jurors who would feel it would be an injustice to send me to prison.

My confidence faded as the deliberations dragged on for four long days. I was beginning to believe that the jurors listened to Judge Hart and they would find me guilty on the facts and the law. In fact, my asshole was so tight by the second day of deliberations you couldn't have driven a nail up it with a sledge hammer.

By the time the jury came back in the court room to render its verdict, I was a nervous wreck. I later learn that there had been one woman on the jury, Carol Holmes, who had been the biggest factor in determining my fate. Carol convinced the other jurors that the right thing to do was find me not guilty and send me home. She had to get all eleven jurors to go along with her and find me not guilty. That's what took four days. If one were to think about it, her actions in that jury room are the reason I'm an attorney today.

I didn't know that the jury had found me not guilty when Carol, as the jury Foreman, stood up and announced the verdict to the courtroom. I couldn't believe my ears when she said in a loud and clear voice, "We the jury, find the defendant, William Harris, not guilty of all charges for which he is accused." That was the moment when I decided that I would be an attorney some day.

After the jury announced my verdict to the court, the D.A. leaned over and buried her face in her hands. Judge Hart thanked the jury for their service and dismissed them. She then turned her iron gaze towards me and spoke these words, "Mr. Harris you are an incredibly lucky young man. You should have been found guilty here today. You should be going to prison for your actions. You might have fooled the jury but you haven't fooled me. I feel certain that even though you're going free today, you will be back in the Criminal Justice System and maybe even back in front of me."

I let out a long sigh after I listened to what the Judge said to me. I didn't want to argue with her, I just wanted to get the hell out of her courtroom and go home. I knew what this trial had done to me. I knew my life would be different now. I was tired when I looked at Judge Hart and said, "Things change."

CHAPTER 17

*I*t is a cold gray miserable winter Monday morning as I leave my duplex and get in my car to make my way to the office. This day matches my mood.

I didn't spend the weekend relaxing or enjoying myself. I am in one of the shittiest moods I have been in since I got out of jail six years ago. Since the day I met John's mother and his sister Dorothy at their home in Belle Meade, my life has become a whirlwind of emotions. I should be in a great mood. Thanks to the fee from John's mother, I have more money in my bank account than I have had since I became a lawyer. Now I don't have to worry as much about coming up with the money to cover Maria's salary.

There I go again thinking about Maria. If it wasn't for her, I might have spent the weekend at Laura's house.

I want to let Maria know that I didn't sleep with Laura, but that might prove to be tricky.

Maria and I don't really have the type of relationship that mandates we account to each other for our personal actions. I know she doesn't have a steady boyfriend. She could have her pick of anybody she wants though. She is just too much of a catch.

I also know that I am not the right man for her. I'm way too old for her. I'm set in my ways. I'm used to being by myself and I'm not sure if I want a relationship even if I wasn't too old for her.

Still, it matters to me that she knows that I didn't sleep with Laura. That is what I am thinking about as I open the door to my office and see Maria sitting at her desk with a small frown on her face. She doesn't seem like she is glad to see me.

Maria usually greets me with a smile in the mornings. Today she's in a tense mood.

The frown on her face gives me an opening to convey my thoughts to her. I look at her and say, "That frown on your face makes me think you must have had the same lousy type of weekend that I did." She looks at me with a perplexed smile on her face and asks me, "What went wrong? I thought you had that big date with Laura?" I roll my eyes and let her know that I didn't sleep with Laura by saying, "Yeah, I stopped by Laura's house for a while but I left early though. I spent the rest of the weekend thinking about John Lester and his damn case. That has left me in a shitty mood for a total of four days now." As soon as I say that, a big grin breaks out on her face. I have to wonder what I said that makes her so happy. I want to know so I ask her, "What's the big grin about?" She giggles to herself a little bit and doesn't answer.

CHAPTER 18

*M*aria is thinking that she is happy to know that William hadn't slept with Laura. She is also more than a little bit happy that he is miserable because of John Lester. She told William not to take John Lester's case and he deserves a bit of grief for not listening to her. Still, she isn't going to let William off the hook. She looks at him with a big grin on her face and says, "Serves you right, I told you John Lester is El Diablo. We don't need his money and you should drop his case right now."

CHAPTER 19

I shake my head while looking at Maria and say, "Too late now, we're in and there is no getting out." Then I ask her, "Anything else going on?" She says, "Yes, there have been five news organizations calling and they want an interview with you. Also, Detective Fowler returned your call and said he will meet with you, so I made an appointment for you to meet him at South precinct this Wednesday, the day before John's preliminary hearing."

I am glad to hear that the Detective has agreed to meet with me. I didn't know if he would agree to a meeting. Meeting with him will be one of the few times, if ever, that I met with a detective when I am sure that I know more about the case than the detective does. Meeting with him on Wednesday is good because it will give me a chance to meet with John on Tuesday. That way, I should be prepared for John's preliminary hearing on Thursday. This afternoon I have to go meet with my old friend, Dakota Gray.

Normally, I would jump at the chance to discuss my case and answer questions for the news media. I have to admit that I like getting my name in the news or seeing myself on television. Not this time though. I want to avoid the media in this case, so I tell Maria, "I'm not going to talk with any reporters about John's case. Tell anyone from the media that there will be no comments."

Maria smiles and says, "What's the matter? You don't want anybody to know you're working for El Diablo?"

I shrug my shoulders and say, "You got that right. Let's

keep John's case to ourselves."

Maria cocks her head sideways, smiles at me as she looks back to the pile of papers sitting on her desk and says, "No problem." I can't believe how much her mood has improved since I got to the office. I don't think I said or did anything to brighten her mood. That gives me more to think about as I make my way to my office.

I am able to get both Maria and John Lester out of my mind for a couple of hours as I concentrate on my other cases. Finally, I am able to get free from the office and go meet Dakota.

CHAPTER 20

*D*akota Gray is my best friend. We've known each other for the last sixteen years.

He is a Marine Corp veteran who did two tours in Afghanistan as a recon Marine. Recon Marines are the soldiers who are tasked with land and amphibious reconnaissance, intelligence collection, surveillance and small unit raids. They straddle the line between special operations forces and conventional forces.

He doesn't talk much about his combat experience in Afghanistan, but I know that he was awarded a bronze star for valor in combat. He is very muscular. He stands about five feet-eleven inches tall. He, like me, has kept himself in good physical condition. Even at our age, Dakota is still nobody to fuck with.

I learned the hard way that he was not to be fucked on the very first day we met. Right after I flunked out of college, I was hanging out with a girl who lived in Lebanon, Tennessee. Lebanon is a small town in Wilson County about twenty-five miles due East of Nashville where Dakota lived then and still lives today. Neither Dakota nor I knew that the girl I was seeing in Lebanon was messing with both of us at the same time.

Something else we didn't know was that she was playing the two of us against each other. One day a few weeks after I started seeing her, her efforts led Dakota and me to the inevitable altercation. Neither one of us fought to gain the affections of the conniving little bitch that set us up to do battle on her behalf. We were fighting for our honor and we were too stupid to back off. The fight started out even enough. I was probably a little over-confident. I had been in numerous fights both in high school and even on the football field when I played in college. From the beginning of the fight to the end the fight, I knew I was overmatched with Dakota. I was able to land a few blows but they didn't seem to faze him. On the other hand, it seemed like every time he landed a blow to my head it put me on my ass. I lost count of how many times he knocked me down when I finally got up for the last time. It took me a while to get up. He waited until I was fully on my feet and facing him before he said to me, "This fight is over. I can't whip you. I would have to kill you to make you stop and I'm not going to do that. Besides, my hands are hurting from hitting you in the head so much." I listened to Dakota and didn't say anything. I stood there staring at him while he stared back at me and then we both started laughing. We've been best friends ever since. I'm not sure what ever happened to the girl.

After that fight, Dakota and I became close and we went almost everywhere together. Neither one of us was ready to settle down. We started frequenting the nightclubs and bars of Nashville on weekends. That's how we got the job working for Billy at Sherry's.

He and I were frequent patrons of Sherry's in those days. We felt fortunate to be allowed in at first. We got into Sherry's with the help of a couple of cocktail waitresses we were seeing who worked in another bar where we hung out. That first night, we went to Sherry's with the waitresses after the bar they worked at closed for the night. We got to know Billy and his doormen. After hanging out there for a while, Billy and the people that worked for him started hanging out with us all of the time. We often left in the morning just as the sun was coming up. Eventually, Billy offered both of us a job one day.

That particular day, Dakota and I were leaving Sherry's just as the sun was coming up. As we opened the door to leave, Billy was standing right outside the front door. He was blocking the way of four menacing looking rednecks who were demanding entry to Sherry's. It was clear to us that he was out numbered, and none of the guys who worked for him were around.

We stood there behind Billy as he told the four rednecks, he was confronting, that Sherry's was a private club and he would decide who he let in. One of the rednecks grabbed him from behind as one of the other three rednecks started to land a punch to his head while he was being held. Before the first guy could land a blow to Billy's head, I threw a punch to the side of one of the other guy's head that put him on his ass. I didn't stop there. As soon as the first redneck hit the ground, I delivered a punch to his buddy standing next to him. It put that bastard on the ground also. While I was taking the two rednecks standing in front of me out of the fight, Dakota was quickly taking care of business with the other two rednecks. He flattened the one that was holding Billy and, within a flash of a second, turned his attention to the other redneck and knocked his ass on the ground with one well-placed punch to his head.

The whole fight lasted no more than twenty seconds from the time we opened the door to leave Sherry's until it was over. The fight ended with Billy, Dakota and I standing with four rednecks lying on the ground around us. There was no more fight left in the rednecks and we let them get up. They scooted off to their cars, never to be seen again.

Billy hired us that night. He fired the two guys who had been working for him, said he couldn't trust them anymore. Billy told us that he needed two guys like us who could take care of business.

We were more than glad to quit our daytime menial jobs for a chance to work at Sherry's. We couldn't have cared less that what we were doing might be slightly illegal. We were having some of the best times of our lives working there. We quickly fell into a pattern of having each other's back in the numerous scuffles and altercations that naturally occur when you're running an establishment like this.

To this day, I know I can count on Dakota to be there for me, no matter what. I know he feels the same way about me.

He stuck with me the whole time I was in jail facing the murder charge. He came to visit me as often as the rules would allow. He even snuck pot in to me in the jail on a couple of occasions. He was in the gallery every day of my trial and was waiting for me at the gate on the day I got out.

After I was free from the murder charge and back on the streets, he quit the nightlife. While I went to college and later law school, Dakota went into the used car business. He is doing very well and is enjoying life too. He has settled down some. He has a steady girlfriend but hasn't proposed.

After I received my law license and started my practice, I talked Dakota into getting his private investigator's license. He didn't need a private investigator's license as a source of income as his used car business was keeping him busy. However, Dakota working with me on my cases as a private investigator gave him a chance to make some extra money and both of us a chance to hang out. It also allows me to discuss confidential details of my client's cases with him. In fact, he helped me on both of the murder cases that I had won for my previous clients.

Dakota turned out to be a natural as a private investigator. He could interview a potential witness and get the most out of that witness, mainly because he is so likable. People are just drawn to him and feel like he can be trusted. The irony of him being a used car dealer is not lost on either of us.

He isn't shy about having to play hardball if the situation requires it. That worked out when Dakota was working as a private investigator for me on my client, A.K.'s, murder case. A.K. had been accused of shooting a guy down in the projects, in cold blood and in plain view of witnesses. The very nature of the case meant that the witnesses were not going to be easy to get to and they would be dangerous as well. To properly prepare the case for trial, Dakota had to go into the gang infested areas of town to talk to potential witnesses. Dakota never backed down. He never even asked me to go with him, although I would have if he had asked.

Dakota just did his job. He went out there and talked to the witnesses. I knew he always took a pistol with him but he never had to pull it during that case. I always felt like it was his winning personality that got him through A.K.'s case with no violence.

When I got my fee on John Lester's case and the extra $25,000.00 for expenses from his family, I called Dakota to let him know that I would need his help as the private investigator. I also let him know that there is $25,000.00 in it for him. We planned to meet and he is expecting to see me today.

As I made the short drive from my office in Old Hickory to Dakota's used car lot in Lebanon, I couldn't help but wonder how he is going to react when I told him how proud John was that he had tortured and killed those three little girls. I wouldn't blame Dakota if he turned this case down but I didn't think he would for a couple of reasons. The first reason being that I am asking for help and the second being that he wouldn't turn down a chance to make $25,000.00. Dakota, like me, appreciates money and he will be more than happy to pocket this fee.

The drive to the dealership went by quickly and I couldn't help but notice, as I turned into the parking lot, that business must be good for him. He probably had fifty to sixty cars on his lot for sale.

Dakota employs three sales reps plus he keeps a full-time receptionist in the office to answer the phone. Business is good and he is thriving.

His office is in the back end of his building. As I walk in the front door, his receptionist waives me on back because she is talking on the phone.

When I walk into his office, his face breaks out into a smile, he stands up, grabs my hand, gives me a hug and says, "Good to see you, old friend. Sit down." Since I started practicing law and he had gotten busy with his car lot, we don't see each other as often as we'd like. I am glad to see him. I wish I didn't have to tell him what John Lester told me a few days before about the murders. I give Dakota a slight smile as I tell him, "You might not feel that way after I give you the facts of this case and what I know about our new client."

Michie Gibson

I tell him everything that John told me about how he tortured and killed those three little girls. I also told him how John had savored the fact that each child died in excruciating pain.

I let Dakota know that, even though John is guilty of these murders, there is a good chance John could take a walk and never be punished for his crimes. I knew Dakota would be bothered by the thought that we might help a psychopath walk free. I want to give him a chance to let me know how he feels about the prospect of helping a sadistic child murderer take a walk and not be punished before he accepts the case. After I explain everything, I look him straight in the eyes and ask him, "If that happens, how would you feel about it and can you live with it?" Dakota looks thoughtful and says, "Not good." Then he asks, "Me living with it, what about you living with it? You know if that mother fucker walks, he will kill again, how do you feel about that?" I look at him and give him the same answer he gave me, "Not good." Then I add, "But don't worry about it. If that happens, I'll figure out how we can live with it. Just trust me. Do you want in?" Dakota doesn't hesitate with his answer, "Sure, you can count me in. What do you want me to do?"

I fill him in on what my client told me went down at his house the night before he was arrested. I explain to Dakota that he needs to find Larry Hargrove and the biker, Wishbone, to prove that Bobby Meyers left Rebecca's panties at John's house. I tell Dakota in no uncertain terms that there is no use looking for Bobby Meyers because I am sure John killed him.

He looks at me and winces when I tell him that Wishbone rides with a motorcycle gang called the Outcasts and Dakota will need to start looking there if he wants to find him.

Dakota says, "That's a tall order. I've heard of the Outcasts - they are nobody to fuck with."

I reply, "Yeah, I know, I've heard of the Outcasts myself. When it comes time to talk to Wishbone let me know and I'll go with you."

Dakota shrugs his shoulders and says, "No problem we'll go see Wishbone together.

Then Dakota chuckles and said, "It could turn out to be fun."

I have to smile when I hear him say that but I have a couple of things I want him to know before I leave. I tell him, "I am going to see John tomorrow. I'm going to tell him your name and that you are working on his case. I don't want you to meet him or for him to see you. That means you don't need to be in court for the preliminary hearing this Thursday either."

Dakota doesn't even bother to ask me why he simply says, "Sure no problem", as I leave.

CHAPTER 21

*I*t's Tuesday afternoon and I'm sitting in the visitor's gallery at CCA, doodling on my notepad, waiting to see John again. I put off going to see him as long as possible.

I spent my morning at the office working on my other cases. While I worked, I couldn't escape the fact that I was going to have to go see him today at some point.

I dread it. I know it is my duty to stay in touch with him as much as possible. The American Bar Association recommends that an attorney whose client is facing the death penalty, visit with that client at least once a week. The thought of having to see the bastard once a week is troubling though. Still, I have no choice since it is vital that I stay in touch with him.

The memory of my last meeting with this asshole is something I will never forget. I have never before been in the presence of a human being that is the essence of pure evil. Even Jack Adams, the man I killed, was not pure evil. Jack basically got himself in a position where the only option left was for me to kill him.

I plan to keep my meeting with John as short as possible. I don't need to hear him gloat about the gruesome details of how he tortured and brutalized the little girls again. I need to get some answers to questions I have. I also know that he probably won't answer all of them. Even so, I have to ask. I would like to know what he did with the panties from the other girls he murdered. I need more information on Wishbone and where I can find John's flunky, Larry Hargrove.

I also need to advise him about what is going on in his

case. He needs to know that I hired Dakota as a private investigator to help me prepare his case for trial. He also needs to know that I scheduled a meeting with the Detective to discuss his case.

My thoughts are cut short as I hear the door that separates the inmates from the visitation area screeching with the sound of metal on metal opening. I watch John as he walks into the room. He doesn't have that look of mayhem, as if he is fixing to beat someone senseless, like he did the first time we met. He does have that shit-eating grin on his face that really pisses me off. It is the same grin that he had after he told me how he murdered those three little girls. God, how I would love to knock that grin right off his face.

John's expression remains the same as he walks over to the table where I am sitting. I don't stand up to greet him or even offer him a handshake. I want to get this meeting over with as soon as possible. He doesn't deserve the courtesy of a handshake.

I can represent John but I am not going to pretend that I like him or exchange pleasantries with him. I keep a blank expression on my face as he approaches.

He sits down and stares at me, still has the grin on his face, and asks me, "Have you been doing your job counselor? I'm getting tired of being locked up." My reply to him is quick, concise and it is the first thought that comes to my mind, "Then you shouldn't have killed anyone." John laughs out loud, "Why not? You killed someone and you're not locked up." His reply catches me by surprise. It is the first time a client of mine has ever mentioned my murder charge.

Before I can reply, his smile quickly turns into a smirk as he speaks to me in a taunting voice that I'm sure is meant to make me angry, "After all, counselor, we are both killers. Why shouldn't I take a walk like you did?"

He is deliberately trying to create tension between us by making me angry. I'm not going to fall into his trap. My answer is short and to the point, "You might take a walk too, I'm work-

Michie Gibson

ing on it."

CHAPTER 22

*J*ohn is disappointed with William's answer. He had hoped to get under his attorney's skin. That thought quickly passes as he digests what William said to him. He is a little surprised that William admitted that he might not be convicted for murdering those three sluts.

John is confident he will not be convicted of killing the girls. Hearing William say it confirms it for him and pleases him.

He loses the grin on his face and is no longer interested in making his attorney lose his cool. He needs to hear why William thinks he might go free.

"What makes you think that?" John asks.

CHAPTER 23

*I*f I could have my way, I would never have told John anything that would give him comfort. I would prefer to bring this asshole all the bad news I can, but that isn't my job. My job is to shoot straight with him and advise him what is helping and what is hurting him.

I think long and hard about his case. He does have a chance to take a walk for these three horrific crimes.

John is right. There is convincing evidence that Bobby Meyers is the one who killed the children. If I do my job correctly, there is a strong possibility that his case can be won. There are a couple of different ways I might pull this off.

I feel like there is a good chance that I might be successful in convincing the jury that Bobby left Rebecca's panties at John's house and that he didn't know anything about them. If that is the case, then John won't be found guilty by a jury.

The other way that John might take a walk for these murders, would be for me to file a Motion to Suppress Rebecca's panties from ever being introduced into evidence at trial.

There is only one way to keep the panties out as evidence at trial. I will have to convince the judge that it will be unfair to my client to let a jury consider them as evidence. Still, it would be at the discretion of the judge whether or not to admit them at trial. If I work hard and am lucky enough to have the judge suppress that evidence, then the government will have a difficult time convicting John of the murder of Rebecca Springer. If the government cannot link my client to those panties, then it has no hope of convicting him for the murders of the other two girls.

Finally, John settles down. He no longer seems intent on baiting me into an argument on the virtues of why I should get to take a walk for killing Jack Adams. I am sure he feels he should also go free for killing the three little girls.

John is right though, we're both killers. I know there is a chance he might take a walk like I did. I also know that my case was different than his. My case is over and it is none of his business and I let him know it.

I tell him, "You're right if everything you told me about Bobby Meyers and Wishbone pans out, then you've got a good chance to go free. I will work hard and do my job and it is my belief and opinion that my efforts will prevent the government from ever punishing you for the murders of those three girls. However, my life is none of your business. I'm here to talk about your case and get some information that I need from you. If you wanna play games then I'm going to get up and walk out of here and withdraw as your attorney of record. I will give your mother's money back. Whatever happens to you after that won't be my problem anymore. But if you want to quit playing games and talk about your case, then there is a strong chance you will take a walk. Just tell me what you want to do."

CHAPTER 24

*A*gain, John is completely put off balance and flustered by William's reaction to his taunting. He was hoping to throw the attorney off his game during the meeting. To John, drama is always fun, he likes making others feel uneasy. He will have to skip it and quit fucking with William. He is more interested in finding out what he needs to do to help beat these murder charges. He is also convinced that his attorney will do what he is required to do. It gives him comfort that William is the exact opposite of him. William is the kind of man you can trust. That's why he is sure William will do what is necessary to persuade a judge, jury or whoever he has to, that Bobby Meyers is the killer. If William does that, John is convinced that he will go free.

"Ok counselor. What do you need from me?", John asks.

CHAPTER 25

I breathe a sigh of relief. Now I can get this meeting with John over and get the hell out of here.

"I've got some questions for you, but first you need to know that I've hired Dakota Gray. Dakota, is a private investigator. He will find Wishbone and Larry Hargrove. Dakota will help me with anything else I need on your case. I'm going to see Detective Fowler tomorrow and find out what he can, or will, tell me about your case."

CHAPTER 26

John is resigned to the realization that this meeting with his attorney is going to be business only. So, he asks William, "What do you want to know?"

CHAPTER 27

I finally relax and ask John my first questions, "How do we find Wishbone? What was he doing at your house the night before Detective Fowler found Rebecca's panties there?"

John starts grinning again as he speaks, "Wishbone hangs out at a biker bar called the Devil's Hangout. You might find him there. But the best place to find Wishbone would most likely be at the Outcasts' clubhouse. I'm not sure where it is. The reason Wishbone was at my house, the night before the cop found the little slut's panties, was to buy stolen guns from Bobby Meyers. Next question."

When I hear this sadistic motherfucker say "little slut's panties" it's all I can do not to gouge his fucking eyes out. Instead I force myself to remain calm on the outside.

"Where can I find Larry Hargrove?" I ask.

John replies, "That will be easy. Larry came to see me the second day I was locked up. He told me about Detective Fowler finding the panties."

John goes on, "I told Larry not to talk to anyone else until he hears from you. He is staying in a transient motel over off Dickerson Pike. He will not answer his mobile number until you text him and let him know it's you. Larry will call you back after you text him. I thought it was best if he talks to you before he speaks to the cops."

John is right about that too. Now that I know how to find Larry, it is crucial that Dakota get to him before the Detective does. I want to make sure that Larry will testify that Bobby Meyers left those panties on John's couch. My hope is that Dakota can interview him before the preliminary hearing. It would be nice if I can get Larry's statement before the hearing.

My time with my client is proving to be more well spent than I thought it would be. I am getting useful information from him that could help his case. I have a few more questions I need to ask John. I also need to let him know what to expect at his preliminary hearing. Maybe I can get out of here soon. I sure hope so.

With the hope of ending this meeting and getting away from this evil presence, my next question is easy. I see no reason that John wouldn't give me an answer. I ask, "In Detective Fowler's report he only mentioned seeing three other cars in your driveway besides your blue Mercedes. If the Camaro is Wishbone's car and I know that the Ford is Larry Hargrove's then was the black Cadillac Bobby Meyers car?"

"Yes", John replies.

I don't think John will answer my next questions but I am still going to ask him, "Where did you kill the three girls? And, what have you done with the other panties that belonged to Patsy Oakley and Tammy Mars?"

John again shakes his head and flashes that shit-eating grin that I hate, as he answers me, "Those are bullshit questions counselor. You don't need to know where those two little sluts' panties are and you don't need to know where I killed them to get me off for their murders. I don't mind telling you though that all three died slowly. It takes a long time to kill a whore the way I do."

John has gotten to me again. I thought I was going to get through this meeting with a couple more questions and a quick explanation of how his preliminary hearing would work. Now all I can think about was the terror and fear that Rebecca, Patsy and Tammy suffered as this sick bastard tortured and killed them.

John knows he has gotten to me. His grin grows into a smirk, while his face is beaming with the satisfaction of a prey animal that has captured its newest victim.

I now feel like John's victim. It is my own fault though. It wasn't necessary for me to ask him any questions about where the two girls' panties are or where he killed all the girls.

John is right, I don't need to know where the other panties are or where he killed the little girls to defend him. I do have a reason for asking him and he needs to know. "You're right, I don't need you to answer those two questions to defend you. I just want to be prepared in the event Detective Fowler stumbles across the murder scene or where you have hidden Patsy and Tammy's panties. But again, you're right, if nothing comes up about it, I can defend you with what I've got. I won't ask again."

CHAPTER 28

John is pleased with himself. William is the only person that he can tell about killing the three sluts. Anyone else would be able to turn him in. William can't because he is his attorney and is sworn to attorney/client confidentiality.

John wishes he could tell more people how he killed the whores. Just telling his attorney how the sluts suffered when he killed them gives him a warm feeling. He relives the high he got from the murders each time he tells William how he watched them suffer before they died. He also gets a kick out of seeing William's look of anxiety. He enjoys the obvious distress on the pompous bastard attorney's face as he gleefully recounts the details of how the girls suffered as he slowly killed them.

William's explanation for why he wants to know where the girls were killed and where John is hiding the other girls' panties tells him a lot about his lawyer. No matter how horrendous the crimes are, or how much his attorney hates him - He will do whatever it takes to make sure John is not convicted for the torture and murders of the three whores. The knowledge that William is working that hard for him, someone he hates, to secure John's freedom for these heinous crimes, while knowing that he is guilty, gives him great pleasure.

John is having fun taunting William with the details of the girls' deaths but he senses that it is time to move on. It is time to let William tell him about the preliminary hearing and what to expect. He firmly feels like he is in control of the meeting now, knowing that his attorney is consumed with the mental image of the girls dying and the way he killed them.

"Ok, fair enough. Tell me what I should expect at my preliminary hearing, counselor."

CHAPTER 29

I am glad the tone of the conversation has calmed down between us. Now, all I have to do to wrap this meeting up is let him know how his preliminary hearing will go. It won't take me but a few minutes to fill him in on the procedure, then I can get the hell out of here.

John listens intently as I explain to him that a preliminary hearing is not the part of the criminal justice process where he will put on his defense. This hearing will be before a General Sessions Judge. The purpose of the hearing is for the District Attorney to convince the Judge that there is probable cause to believe that John killed the three girls and bind his case over to the Grand Jury. I tell John that, more than likely, the only person who will testify for the government tomorrow will be Detective Fowler.

When I tell John that, he looks at me with his eyes wide open and asks me, "When will I testify?"

His question catches me by surprise. It never occurred to me that he would think he is going to testify after he confessed to me that he killed the three girls. Still, it doesn't take but a second for me to answer, "You never will," I tell him, "you can't."

My answer to John's question infuriates him so much that he glares at me as he leans in toward me. His face is so close to mine that the only thing separating us is the table where we are sitting. John yells, "Why the hell wouldn't I testify? The jury needs to hear me say that I have no idea how that little slut's panties got in my house. They are going to hear Larry and Wishbone say how the panties got to my house without my know-

116

ledge, not to mention the fact that you should be able to figure out how to prove that Bobby Meyers has a fetish for little girls' panties. There is no way a jury can find me guilty. There is no reason for me not to testify."

I have a good explanation for him on why he won't testify. First, I have to let him know in no uncertain terms that he crossed the boundary again by yelling in my face. I lean forward so close that our noses are within a couple of inches of each other. I am staring straight into his evil eyes as I tell him, in a threatening voice that only the two of us are able to hear, "You best back off motherfucker or I will hurt you really bad."

CHAPTER 30

*J*ohn is furious with himself. Once again, he is terrified by his attorney. He didn't mean to scream at William and get in his face. The memory of how William scared him the first time they met is still fresh in his mind. He had gotten so mad when William told him he wasn't going to testify, that he lunged at him without thinking.

John is terrified but he doesn't believe William is going to hurt him. He sits back, softens his voice along with his attitude and simply asks, "Why can't I testify?"

CHAPTER 31

I am glad John has calmed down. I also know that I have scared him. Knowing that makes me smile a little as I explain to him that he can't testify because he told me what he did to the girls. I tell him I can't let him testify now that I know the truth. Letting him testify would be unethical on my part. I cannot allow him to get on the stand and lie. He needs to know that even if he were to fire me and hire another attorney, any new attorney will know that he confessed to me that he is guilty of the murders. Because of that, his new attorney wouldn't let him testify either.

With that explanation, I say to John, "You might as well get used to the idea you're never going to testify. I don't think it will make any difference though. I don't think you will ever be punished by the government for killing those three children, whether you testify or not. We have enough honest testimony and facts to work with. Even without you lying, you will more than likely be set free anyway."

John listens to everything I tell him, then asks me, "Why do you care if I take the stand and lie? Nobody will know that I'm lying but us two. If I testify it would make sure you win my case. Think of all the publicity you will get."

"I care because I took an oath to obey the laws and rules of the land. If I allow you to testify when I know that your testimony is false, that's called subornation of perjury and I can't do that. I won't break the rules for you. You shouldn't worry though; I feel confident you will go free without testifying"

He doesn't reply to anything I say to him. I take his moment of silence to say one last thing before I get up to leave, "Just sit tight and let me do my job.

CHAPTER 32

*J*ohn is back sitting in his cell contemplating how his meeting with William went. The way he looks at it, the time spent with his attorney had been encouraging in many ways.

He is sure that William will do what it takes to set him free.

He knows that the private investigator will find Wishbone. Finding Wishbone is crucial to him walking out of jail a free man. Wishbone has to testify that Bobby Meyers brought the panties to his house.

He knows how to control William. Controlling the attorney proved to be easy. A man like William Harris is bound by his own sense of honesty and ethics. That's why he knows that William will do what is necessary to set him free. William is bound by his own honesty which forces him to do the right thing and defend John zealously within the bounds of the law.

John has made it easy for him to defend him within the bounds of the law. He carefully manipulated the evidence and the proof so a jury or a judge could not help but think that Bobby Meyers is the person that most likely killed the three little sluts.

William has no choice but to let Wishbone and Larry Hargrove testify because he knows that both of them will be telling the truth.

The idea that his attorney will put this proof and evidence before a judge or jury amuses him.

The thought of how his case is fucking with William's mind is a comforting way to ease the burden of being locked up.

He knows William hates him. It is ironic that William despises him but still has to defend him and eventually see him set free.

When he isn't amusing himself with thoughts of how his case is making his attorney miserable, his thoughts turn elsewhere. Late at night when everyone is in their cells asleep, he relives the pleasure of torturing and killing the three sluts. He gets an erection thinking about how each girl tried to scream but couldn't because he stuffed their panties in their mouths.

John loves killing. He has no remorse for the girls or the animals he's killed.

He wants to get out of this cell. He is tired and bored of being in a cage. He has underestimated how hard living behind bars would be. He wants to get back to his farm. He isn't worried that someone will find his trophy room there or Bobby's body rotting in a shed out behind the cabin. The place is too well hidden. He needs to get back to his trophy room. He desperately desires to caress the dead girls' panties one more time.

He will eventually have to destroy his trophy room and dispose of Bobby's body then move on. It is too risky for John in Nashville, maybe even in the United States, to continue his love of killing young girls.

Being locked up gives him the time to think about what his next move will be after he is free. As soon as possible, he is going to kill again. He will be more careful from now on though.

John won't kill again until he is certain he will not get caught.

Even though he is having fun framing Bobby for the girls he murdered. The fun he was having is not worth being locked up in this cage.

When he gets out, John plans to wait on his mother to die. He is sure he can control his desire to kill until then.

When the old bag dies, he will inherit hundreds of millions of dollars. He will move to another country where the law can be paid to look the other way if young girls go missing. He has done the research and there are countries in South America where he can live in a luxurious villa and hire thugs to protect him. His employees will even bring him the young girls he craves. With the money he will inherit he won't have to worry about interference from the law in those countries.

John misses killing. He wants to get out of jail, leave the country and kill again.

First, he has to be set free for murdering these girls. That means he has to work with his attorney. Working with William calls for him not to lose his cool like he had when his attorney told him he wouldn't let him testify. He is going to make sure he never interacts with William in a manner that provokes his anger again. William has now terrified John twice and John doesn't want that to ever happen again.

All he needs to do is sit tight. William will get him off for these three murders. Maybe he will get a chance to kill his attorney then. That is something to think about. His attorney is on his list now.

CHAPTER 33

*I*t is Wednesday afternoon and outside it is bitter cold with a hint of snowflakes in the air. I'm on my way to the Nashville South Police Precinct to keep my appointment with Detective Fowler.

Even though I have never met this Detective before now, I am familiar with his reputation. He is known as a maverick for bucking the powers that be if he thinks it is necessary to make his case. I am curious why he agreed to meet with me. He doesn't have to. His meeting with me won't help the government's case against John.

My meeting with John yesterday proved beneficial to putting one of the necessary pieces together that will help me in providing a successful defense for him. I contacted Larry Hargrove with the instructions that John gave me for setting up a meeting with he and Dakota Gray. Dakota met with Larry and was able to record Larry's statement that he was at John's house the night before Detective Fowler found Rebecca Springers' panties there. That John had smacked Bobby Meyers in the head and that Bobby told John he would get even with John someday. Dakota assured me that he was confident that Larry would not talk to anyone from the police department. Dakota let me know that John trained Larry well. John gave Larry strict instructions to stay hidden and not talk to anyone until he was contacted by the attorney representing John. Dakota said Larry was grateful to hear from us and wanted to go home.

Now that Larry's testimony is nailed down, the next piece in the puzzle is finding Wishbone and securing his testimony. Finding Wishbone wasn't going to be as easy as finding Larry was plus it would have to wait.

I will let Detective Fowler know that I have found Larry Hargrove. I will also let him know that Larry will not talk to him but he is welcome to try. I have to play it closer to the vest when discussing Wishbone with the Detective though. I don't think he knows who Wishbone is or that Wishbone was at John's house the night before he found Rebecca's panties there. It's important that either Dakota or I find Wishbone before the police do. Nailing down Wishbone's testimony and making sure he testifies truthfully is my best hope. It is also my greatest challenge in successfully defending John.

These are my thoughts as I step out into the bitter cold and make my way through security where I am directed to an office door marked "Detectives - Homicide Division - South Precinct - Nashville Tennessee" in bold black letters above the door. The officer at the front desk takes me back to where Detective Fowler.

The Detective stands up and we shake hands as the officer leaves us alone in the room.

He is close to my age. He has a slim build and is almost my height. His hair is thick and blond, sprinkled heavily with gray. His face is neutral as he greets me. I get the distinct feeling that this is his normal facial expression.

"I sure appreciate you meeting with me Detective. I know you didn't have to," I tell him as we sit down on opposite sides of his desk.

"Yes, I did", is his quick response.

I feel sure I know what he means with his answer and I acknowledge as much with my question, "Bob Lyons?"

Detective Fowler is one of many police officers who had opposed the government charging me with felony murder for killing Jack Adams. He is letting me know that I earned the privilege of a face to face meeting when I saved his fellow officer's life.

I nod my head and ask Detective Fowler, "Is Bob a friend of

yours?"

Detective Fowler says, "More than a friend, we went through the academy as rookies. His family and mine vacation together. I'm godfather to Bob's only child. I never got a chance to thank you for saving my best friend's life, so I'm doing it now. Thank you."

His demeanor never changed as he talked. He maintained that same icy stare as he thanked me in a quiet voice that I had to listen to carefully, in order to make sure I catch everything he said. I would bet dollars to donuts that this is the same tone of voice and icy stare that has unnerved many of the potential suspects that he has interviewed in his career.

As I listen to him thank me for saving his best friend's life, his facial expression hasn't change from the first moment I met him. I know from that moment on he and I will have a special relationship even though we might not be the closest of buddies. The simple fact that he thanked me meant we were cut from the same cloth. Detective Fowler is a man that will do the right thing no matter what the consequences. From now till the day I die I am certain that he is the type of man I can trust. I also feel certain that he knows that John is guilty.

"No problem, I'm sure you would have done the same thing if you had been in my shoes." I replied.

Detective Fowler didn't say anything but the little smile out of the corner of his mouth told me everything I needed to know about him.

He loses his slight smile as he stares at me and says, addressing me by my first name, "William, I like you but I have serious problems with your client and I'm going to do everything that I can to see that he goes down. I also know that John Lester is guilty. I know you know it too. And please do me a favor, call me Randy not Detective Fowler."

I let out a sigh when I hear him clue me in that I am not going to fool him into believing I think John is innocent. I never intended to let him know that I know my client is guilty. Our meeting is more for my benefit than the government's. I need to know whether or not he knows who Wishbone is and, if he does, whether or not he is any closer to finding him than I am.

I shake my head and tell him, "Randy, I'm sure I know a lot more about John Lester than I am able to or even care to talk about with you. I'm not here to help the government convict John no matter what I think or know about him. That's not my job. I know you understand that. I can help you with one thing though. I know where Larry Hargrove is but I doubt he will talk to you."

As he replies to me, Randy's facial expression and demeanor return to the same icy stare he had when I first sat down, "I understand William, if you have to play it that way. Not sure if I could do it. John Lester needs to be punished and you know I'm right but it's your ballpark. I'll look up Larry Hargrove, I've been wanting to talk with him. Sounds like it won't do me any good though but I've still got to try. Is there anything else you got for me?"

"Yes, I saw in your report that you saw three cars, besides John's, in John's driveway when you drove by his house the night before you found Rebecca Springer's panties. Do you know who was driving in the other two cars?" I ask him.

Randy lets out a long sigh, rolls his head back and closes his eyes as he replies, "No, I don't know the owner of those cars. I couldn't make out the tags and I was in a hurry. I bet you know who owns the cars and you're not going to tell me." He says, with a hint of sarcasm in his voice.

My reply to Randy is quick and to the point, "Yes, I do know the owner of the black Cadillac. Bobby Meyers is the name of the owner of that car. I am still getting the name of the owner of the Camaro. All I have now is an alias, and you're right, I can't tell you."

I can tell he is starting to worry that somehow John is going to use me to find a way of never being punished by the government for killing the three girls. I have heard that he took a chance on being demoted for even pursuing John as a suspect. I don't want to bullshit him but I can't tell him that Wishbone owns the Camaro and protect John's rights.

So, I give him the best answer I can, "Look, I know you are a good cop. I know you have seen close up what the man who killed those three little girls did to them before they died. I know you are sure John Lester is the man who killed them. You're probably right about that. But I think it's only fair that you know that I believe there is more than a little chance that the government might not be able to convict him, even if he is guilty. John going free all depends on me doing my job and getting a little luck. Don't forget that him going free depends on whether or not I find the owner of the Camaro before you do."

The Detective listens to everything I tell him. He takes his time before he speaks to me and says, "William, I will always owe you. When you killed Jack Adams, you saved my best friend's life. I know Bob is grateful you saved his life as well. I would have handled it differently if it had been my life you saved that night."

As I get up to leave, I casually ask, "Oh yeah, what would you have done differently than Bob did?"

His answer gives me a lot to think about as I am leaving. "I would have cut you lose before backup came on the scene. You would never have been arrested."

CHAPTER 34

*S*even days have come and gone since I first laid eyes on John Lester. Over the past seven days he has become a fixture in my life. My previous clients didn't linger in my thoughts once their cases are over. That isn't going to happen with this case. No matter how his case ends, I know I will never completely erase John and what he did to those little girls from my thoughts. In the years to come, the memories of this case will creep into my thoughts at times when such thoughts of horror would be least expected. It never occurred to me when John's mother paid me to represent him that I would become a slave to the memories of his crimes and would be shackled to thoughts of how he brutalized those girls before he killed them.

It's Thursday morning and I'm at the Justice A. A Birch Building in downtown Nashville at the Davidson County Criminal Court where John's preliminary hearing is to take place.

As I enter the building, I notice numerous vehicles from the media parked out front. I can only assume that they are here for John's hearing. I ride the elevator up to the fifth floor where the preliminary hearing is set to take place. The elevator doors open and it is obvious that all the news vans parked out front are here for this case. As soon as the elevator doors open, one of the reporters recognizes me and rushes me with a microphone in her hand. She is soon followed by a score of other reporters who see me exit the elevator. They are following her lead hoping to get a sound bite from me about the case that they can play later on the news tonight.

I have never shied away from TV cameras before but this

case is different. I don't plan to make a statement for the benefit of the viewing public on tonight's news cast. As the throng of reporters surround me, I make what I hope will be my last and only statement to the press, "There will be no comments from the defense at this time or at any time in the future." Having said that, I gently and slowly push my way through the reporters towards the courtroom door.

As I break through the crowd, the first person I see is Laura Kincaid. She is standing next to the door leading into the courtroom, smiling at me. Laura looks great. She is dressed conservatively, wearing navy blue slacks and jacket with a light blue silky blouse.

This is the first time we have seen each other since I was at her house a week ago. I don't know how to read her smile.

Is she smiling at me because I am a fool - a fool who might have had one of the best nights of his life with her, but passed? Or, is she smiling for another reason? It's good to see her as I make my way to where she is standing so we can talk in private.

She never lost that smile as I approach her. "You having fun yet cowboy?", she asks.

This is the second time she has called me cowboy. I won't say I don't like it. It sounds sexy the way she says it. Still, I don't think the name fits me. I'm not a cowboy. "So," I ask her, "why do you call me cowboy?"

"Well you do wear boots with your suits. That's not the reason I think of you as a cowboy though." Laura says.

"What is it then?", I ask.

"In my romantic mind, you're the perfect picture of what I think a cowboy symbolizes, the kind of cowboy you see in those old black and white movies. I think you possess great courage. When I'm with you I feel safe. You have a tendency to not think out what you're doing and that gets you in trouble. For some reason, you always land on your feet and skip the serious consequences for your actions. You either have dumb luck or maybe you're in God's good graces for some reason. But, most of all, you seem like the kind of cowboy that can be trusted to do the right thing, no matter what the consequences. That cowboy, is why I think I may be falling in love with you." Laura speaks these words to me with a gleam in her eyes. She then turns and enters the courtroom. Leaving me standing there alone.

Damn! Now I have more to think about than John's preliminary hearing. The night I left Laura's house and declined her invitation to sleep with her, I didn't have any idea how she would act the next time we met. After that night, it wouldn't surprise me if she never spoke to me again.

Now, she is telling me the door to her bedroom is still open if I want to come in. Still, it feels like a commitment though and I'm not sure if I am ready for that.

Not only that, why in the hell did she pick now of all times to drop that bombshell on me. It's not like I have time to react to what she said, much less think about it.

My mind is buzzing as I turn back to face the hallway when I see Dorothy Lester with her mother standing beside her. They have their backs against the wall.

I quickly approach them and speak to the two of them. I say, with a slight smile on my face, "Good morning. I didn't see you guys when I got off the elevator. Is everything ok?"

Dorothy speaks for the two of them, "We saw you get off the elevator and how you were mobbed by those reporters. They have been harassing us too. I noticed you didn't give a statement. Why not?"

My answer to her is quick and short, "Didn't want to."

She frowns at my answer, which makes me think she might not be pleased with my response, when she asks me, "Got any suggestions on how we can avoid the reporters?"

Her question suddenly makes it clear to me that I need to add shielding her and her mother from the hordes of reporters to my to do list for today. I feel like neither one of them deserves to be in that courtroom. John's crimes have had way more impact on their lives than mine.

Dorothy, who had seemed so self-confident and had such

determination the few times I met her, now seems over-whelmed and lost by all that is going on.

I present them with the best plan I can come up with. "I think the judge will take John's case first. The reporters prob-ably want to leave as soon as they can after the hearing. I'll walk you both into the courtroom now and you can go ahead and take a seat. The reporters won't harass you while you are sitting in court. After the hearing is finished, the three of us will wait for a little while before we leave the courtroom. I expect all of the reporters should be gone by then. When we leave, I'll walk the two of you to your car."

As I am explaining this to them, Mrs. Lester tears up and asks me, "Mr. Harris, if there is any way possible that you can get John free, will you do that? Can you make me that promise? I love him more than you can imagine and I couldn't go on living if he has to live in a cage the rest of his life or if they kill him."

Dorothy bites her lip when she hears her mother's ques-tion to me. She is obviously distraught that her mother is cry-ing and gently begging me to save her only son's life. I know how she feels about her brother. Even so, that doesn't stop her from taking her mother's hand as I answer Mrs. Lester's question hon-estly, "Mrs. Lester, I don't have all the answers. I can't make any promises. But I believe there is a good chance your son will walk free and never be executed."

Evidently, my answer gives her some instant relief. I can see it on her face. Dorothy's reaction to my assertion that there is a good chance John might go free is dramatically different than her mother's. As I spoke, Dorothy's head jerks back and her eyes open wide with a look of total astonishment and shock. I am sure that she doesn't want to hear that.

She needs to face the reality that her brother may go free and probably will, if this case goes the way I think it will.

Dorothy has a somber look on her face as I hold the door to the courtroom open and follow them in.

The cameras are already set up in the courtroom and each camera is trained on the three of us as we make our entrance.

The victim witness coordinator from the District Attorney's Office is sitting beside three middle aged couples. They are directly behind the desk where the Assistant District Attorney will sit. The only thing that separates the three couples from the desk is a short wooden barrier called the bar. These six people are the parents of the girls that my client tortured and murdered.

I recognize Rebecca Springer's parents from the news. Rebecca's father didn't hold back his thoughts when talking to the reporters after John was arrested. He let the world know that John didn't deserve a trial and that he should suffer the same grizzly death his little girl had. I can't say that I blame him.

After Dorothy and her mother sit down, Rebecca's father continues to glare at them. He only quits glaring at them when I leave the two of them sitting in the gallery on a bench in the back of the courtroom. As I make my way to the desk where Lindsey Moreland, the Assistant District Attorney, and Detective Fowler are sitting, Rebecca's father shifts his glare to me and follows my footsteps. His eyes are filled with hatred for the attorney representing the man who tortured and killed his little girl. I can find no fault in Rebecca's father hating me. I don't blame him for that. I ignore his stare and make sure we never make eye contact. I want to avoid Rebecca's father at all costs. I can tell he is on the verge of exploding and I am determined not to do anything to provoke him.

The D. A. and I have seen each other in the halls and rooms of the courthouse from time to time since I have become an attorney. However, this is my first case with her as the prosecuting attorney and me defending someone besides myself. In the two years that I have been practicing law, we have never talked to one another. I'm sure that she, like me, thinks of our previous trial every time we cross paths. Lindsey is medium height with an average build, has short dark blonde hair and is easy to look at. She has a no non-sense attitude and is a very good attorney.

She smiles at me as I approach her and the Detective. Lindsey says to me, "William, it looks like we have our second case together where we are opposing counsel in a murder case. I'm thinking I'll get a better a result this time than I did the last time. " She pauses and nods her head towards Randy and says, "I believe you already met Detective Fowler."

She adds, "You know your client is guilty and I don't think you are going to be able to help him."

I give her a quick and short answer, "Just being guilty doesn't mean he will be convicted."

She doesn't have time to respond before the bailiff calls out for quiet in the courtroom and for everyone to stand for Diane Turner, the General Sessions Judge. The Judge enters and takes her seat at the bench. I sit down and wait for the docket call to finish so we can begin.

CHAPTER 35

*J*ohn is sitting in the holding cell that is adjacent to the courtroom waiting for his preliminary hearing to start. He is in an elated mood.

He should be in a foul mood. The crowded bus ride from CCA to the courthouse early this morning was cramped, stank of piss and vomit, and made him want to throw up. Now he is sitting in this small dark grey holding cell, that smells exactly like the bus, waiting for his name to be called.

Still, he is in a great mood. Unlike everyone else in this holding cell, he knows he will eventually go free and not be punished for his crimes. He is certain his attorney will find Wishbone so he doesn't have much to worry about.

John is in a hurry for the bailiff to call his name, then he will know that his preliminary hearing is starting. The first thing he is going to do when he enters the courtroom is locate the parents of the three dead little sluts. The thought that he will be within a few feet of their mothers and fathers excites him. Knowing that gives him an erection. So much so, that when his name is called, he has trouble hiding his excitement as he stands up to walk into the courtroom.

He enters the courtroom from a side door that leads to the holding cells. As he walks in the room, he sees William sitting at a desk on the left facing the Judge. He recognizes the Assistant District Attorney and Detective Fowler from the news. They are sitting at a desk on the right facing the Judge. Between the two desks is a podium, behind which attorneys stand, as they question a witness. The witnesses that will be testifying will sit in a chair by the judge. John made himself familiar with how the courtroom is laid out and where everyone will be sitting. His purpose for learning the layout of the courtroom was to enable him to almost immediately zero in on where the girls' parents are sitting.

He is pleased with himself because he spots them before he reaches the defense table. The parents of the three girls are sitting on a bench directly behind the D.A. and Detective.

He makes sure all the parents are looking directly at him. When he catches their eye, he smiles and blows them a kiss.

You can hear an audible gasp from the people sitting in the gallery when he blew the kiss at the parents. Their mummers are drowned out by the scream of Rebecca's father, "You motherfucker! I'll kill you for what you did to my baby girl!", as he jumps up from his seat and lunges at John. John's grin turns into an outright laugh as he watches the court officers tackle Rebecca's father before he can get close enough to even touch John, much less strike him. As the court officers drag Rebecca's father out of the courtroom, John quickly sits down at the desk with his attorney while calmly turning his head to face the Judge.

CHAPTER 36

I am sitting at the defense desk when I hear a scream coming from somewhere behind. John is next to me. I turn around in time to see the court officers tackle Rebecca's father and drag him out of the courtroom. After the commotion dies down, I lean over to John and whisper to him. "You have any idea what that was about?"

John, who is now sitting perfectly still with his hands folded together in front of him looking straight ahead, shakes his head and says, "I haven't got a clue."

Once the court officers remove Rebecca's father from the courtroom, I turn my attention back to Judge Turner who is banging her gavel and ordering the courtroom to be quiet or she will clear the room.

The noise quickly dies down after the Judge let everyone in the courtroom know that she is in control and wasn't going to mess around. If you want to remain in her domain you will play by her rules. While the judge is talking, I quietly wait for the D.A. to call Detective Fowler as the first witness.

I am in trial mode and had no idea that John had blown a kiss to the dead girls' parents until after the hearing. The video of him blowing a kiss at the murdered girls' parents is a news clip that is shown repeatedly on both local and national news outlets for days to come.

I watch as Detective Fowler takes the stand. He is self-confident and calm while answering the D.A.'s questions. He acted the same way yesterday when I met with him at the police precinct.

Randy's testimony offers no new details or facts that I am not already aware of. He testifies that he had developed John as a person of interest for the girls' murders on a hunch. He didn't have evidence to link my client to the murders until he stopped by John's house and saw the panties laying in plain view. He said that after he saw the panties, Larry Hargrove voluntarily gave the panties to him.

Randy's testimony ends with him explaining to Judge Turner that he took the panties found in John's home to his superiors and asked that the forensic lab put a rush on the testing. He testifies that DNA from those panties, found on John's couch, matched Rebecca Springer's DNA. He then arrested John Lester for the murders of the three girls. His reasoning for charging him with the murders of Patsy Oakley and Tammy Mars was that their murders were so similar to Rebecca's that it is obvious that the same person murdered all three girls.

Lindsey thanks him for his testimony, then it is my turn to cross examine him. I don't have many questions for Randy to answer. I know that his testimony establishes probable cause for John's case to be bound over to Criminal Court. I need to establish facts that will help me defend John when his case gets transferred to Criminal Court. I also will obey the unwritten rule that was drilled in my head from my first year in law school. That rule is that any lawyer worth his salt never asks a witness a question that the lawyer doesn't know the answer to.

My meeting with Randy yesterday established facts that will help me defend my client. The Detective's answers in court today will confirm those facts. Through his testimony, I need to establish that there were three cars parked in John's driveway that night, besides the blue Mercedes. Bobby Meyers owns the black Cadillac; Larry Hargrove owns the red Ford; and that the police don't know who owns the Camaro. I also want him to acknowledge that, not only did the lab test reveal that Rebecca Springer's DNA was found on those panties, but the test results also disclosed the presence of unknown DNA.

Since I know what Randy's answers to my questions will

be, my job is to frame my questions to him in a manner that suggests the answers I need. The Detective will have no other choice than to respond by simply saying - yes - when answering my questions.

Once I have the answers I need on the record, I will have all the facts necessary to file a motion to suppress the panties. If successful, that motion will exclude the panties from being used as evidence when this case is bound over to Criminal Court by Judge Turner today.

With that in mind, I ask Randy my first question. "Detective Fowler, you and I met yesterday and during that meeting the two of us established some facts that the both of us agree on. Isn't that correct?"

Randy nods his head slightly and says, "You're right, we did counselor."

"And isn't it true that you drove by John Lester's home the night before you found Rebecca Springer's panties on my client's couch?"

He simply replies, "Yes."

"It's also true that you saw four cars that same night sitting in John Lester's driveway?" I ask.

Again, Randy nods his head when he answers, "Yes."

It is important that I put into the record, through the Detective's testimony, how many cars were in John's driveway that night. I also want to establish that Bobby Meyers was at John's house and that Bobby is the owner of the black Cadillac. I will link the facts that Bobby Meyers was at John's house and had left Rebecca's panties there that night when I find Wishbone and have him testify later.

"There was a blue Mercedes that belonged to my client, a red Ford, a black Cadillac, and a Chevy Camaro, isn't that correct Detective Fowler?" I ask.

"Yes", answers Randy.

"When we met yesterday, I believe you told me that those were the three cars in John's driveway, besides John Lester's blue Mercedes, the night you drove by my client's house? Isn't that correct Detective Fowler?"

He replies simply, "Yes."

"Isn't it correct that you told me, when we met yesterday, that you recognized the red Ford as a car that belongs to Larry Hargrove and you weren't able to determine who owns the black Cadillac or the Camaro that were parked in John Lester's driveway?" I ask Randy.

"That's correct", Randy states.

I am getting exactly what I expect and want from Randy's answers. Now I need for him to testify that I gave him Bobby Meyers' name as the owner of the black Cadillac he saw that night. I will then question him to determine if he followed up on my tip that Bobby owns the black Cadillac.

"Detective Fowler I gave you the name of Bobby Meyers as the individual who owns the black Cadillac you saw in my client's driveway on the night in question. Did you have a chance to check that out?" Randy's answer provides me with more information than I expect but is exactly what I want to hear when he testifies.

"Based on the information you provided to me yesterday, I was able to search Bobby Meyers' name in our data bank. Mr. Meyers has a criminal record for several theft charges. I was also able to determine that Bobby Meyers does own a black Cadillac. I located the address where he lives here in Nashville. I went to that address and knocked on the door to his apartment. No one answered, but I did observe the black Cadillac in the parking lot. I determined the black Cadillac was the same black Cadillac I had observed in John Lester's driveway the night I drove by his house. The vehicle has the same damage to the right back quarter-panel that I observed before. Based on that new evidence, I am in the process of obtaining a search warrant for Bobby Meyers' apartment. I also impounded the black Cadillac."

His testimony is a mixed bag of good news for me to sort out. It is no surprise that Randy confirmed that Bobby Meyers' black Cadillac was in John's driveway the night in question. I was sure the Detective would follow up my lead that Bobby

Meyers was one of the individuals at John's house the night Randy drove by. His added testimony, that he is in the process of obtaining a search warrant for Bobby Meyers apartment, is great news for me. He will search Bobby Meyers' apartment where he will find Bobby's collection of panties.

Finding a collection of panties in Bobby's apartment will strengthen my argument. I will be able to convince a judge that it would be unfair to allow Rebecca's panties to be introduced into evidence to convict my client. All the pieces to successfully defending John are falling into place for me.

All that is left for me to obtain from the Detective's testimony concerns Rebecca's panties and the lab results. Then I will be done with my questions.

"Detective Fowler, you testified here today that the lab results that were done on the panties you found at my client's home showed trace DNA that matched the DNA of Rebecca Springer. Was there evidence of anyone else's DNA found on those panties?" I ask.

"Yes, there were traces of an unknown person's DNA detected on the panties that came from John Lester's house." he answers.

That is it. I have everything I need. I have much more than I hoped for from the testimony. I thank him for his testimony then close my proof. I sit down and wait for Judge Turner to rule on whether or not there is sufficient probable cause to bound the case over to Criminal Court. I know there will be. There usually is in these cases no matter what comes out in the preliminary hearing. The fact that a preliminary hearing is the State's time to put forth its case and not the defense's, means getting bound over is typically the outcome.

Judge Turner wastes no time ruling that she finds sufficient evidence to send John's case to Criminal Court. As soon as she rules, the guards take my client back to the holding cell. I walk to the back of the courtroom where I told Dorothy and her mother to sit and wait for me earlier.

She and her mother are where I left them. Mrs. Lester is

gently crying while Dorothy embraces her. I sit next to the two of them as we wait for enough time to pass to give the reporters a chance to clear out so I can walk them to where their car is parked.

CHAPTER 37

*M*y plan worked. There are no reporters in the halls or outside the courthouse as I shepherd Dorothy and her mother to their car. They had parked across the street from the courthouse in an underground garage. We cross the busy street and ride the elevator down to the fifth floor of the garage. As we approach their car, I notice an old Chevy Malibu that looks like it has seen better days parked next to Dorothy's Lexus. The hood is up on the Chevy, with a man bent over peering into the engine compartment. He has his back turned to us as we approach.

When we get close enough that the man can hear us walking, he stands up and turns to face us. I am surprised to see that it's Rebecca's father and my first thought is, "Oh shit!"

I can almost feel Mr. Springer's pain and anger. I am aware that the reality of what had happened to Rebecca and the thought of his daughter dying alone with such cruelty is driving his emotions to the point it is impossible for him to think rationally. At that point, I still didn't know that John had blown the parents a kiss as he was sitting down.

I didn't learn about that bullshit until later that night when I, like millions of other people, first saw it on the local news and then on the national news. Knowing that wouldn't have made any difference about what I thought was the best way to handle this situation.

Even though Mr. Springer is driven to such a savage rage that he is out of control, I don't perceive him as a threat to us. He isn't a big man, probably about five feet-eight inches tall with a slight build.

I need to get Dorothy and Mrs. Lester into their car as quickly as possible. Hopefully, we can avoid this awkward encounter by my keeping them away from Mr. Springer. I hope this chance meeting will pass with no harsh words or threats of violence coming from Mr. Springer. It is not to be though.

Before the three of us are able to get to Dorothy's car, Mr. Springer's wife gets out of their car to stand beside her husband. His wife standing beside him seems to embolden Mr. Springer. He takes a threatening step towards Mrs. Lester, screaming at her, "You filthy whore! I bet you're proud of your boy now! I bet it makes you feel really good when you hear how your boy tortured my Rebecca before she died!"

I sympathize with Mr. Springer's agony, but this has gone far enough. Mrs. Lester is sobbing uncontrollably and has a terrified look on her face. Dorothy wraps her arms around her mother and hugs her tightly as she puts herself between her mother and Mr. Springer. Dorothy is attempting to shield her mother from Mr. Springer's wrath.

I step between them with both my arms stretched up by my head and with my hands open, I yell, "Stop! That's enough!"

My words have no effect on Mr. Springer. He slows down but does not stop advancing in the direction of Dorothy and Mrs. Lester as he growls at me. "Get out of my way you son of a bitch." Before I know it, he hits me in the side of my head, right above my chin, on my jaw bone. Mr. Springer's punch isn't the type of blow that is so devastating that it could end a fight. But still the blow to my head stings and gets my attention. My hope is that I still may be able to end this encounter with Mr. Springer without letting the situation escalate out of control.

I don't want it to go any further than it already has. I step back a couple of steps, still facing him, while leaving my hands in the air and again I yell, "Stop! That's enough!"

Once more, my words have no effect on Mr. Springer as he continues to advance and growls at me, "I told you to get out of my way." Then he lands another blow to my head. Damn, he hit me in almost the same spot he hit me before.

I take two more steps back, but this time I don't hold my hands up in the air. Instead, I put both arms straight out in front of my body, with my hands outstretched and resting on Mr. Springer's shoulders. This prevents him from advancing any further. I lower my voice and lean in close to him. I am staring directly into his eyes when I say, "I will not let you go any further. You won't get the benefit of another unanswered blow to my head. I realize this day has been one of the worst days of your life. But if you try to move any closer to these two ladies, I promise you that this will end badly for you. Please do us both a favor and go stand by your wife while they get into their car and leave."

Mr. Springer listens to what I say, he doesn't try to push his way past me, but he isn't retreating either.

It looks like my words to him aren't going to stop this situation from going to the next level. Finally, I hear Mr. Springer's wife cry out to him, "Roger do as the man asks. Come stand beside me." I didn't know Mr. Springer's first name until now.

Roger pauses and looks at me. Tears are starting to roll down his cheeks. He drops his head, turns and takes the few steps that are separating him from his wife and stands beside her as she takes his hand in hers.

I direct Dorothy and Mrs. Lester to get in their car. I take the driver's seat in order to drive the three of us out of the garage to the main street above. As I drive away, I glance in the rear-view mirror to see Roger and his wife holding hands and sobbing as we leave the garage.

CHAPTER 38

*I*t is late July. The weather is sunny and pleasant. My mood doesn't match the great weather we are having.

I'm sitting at my desk reading a subpoena with my name on it. I, along with the D.A., Lindsey, have been summoned by Judge Hart to discuss scheduling dates for John's murder cases. The subpoena is Judge Hart's message letting us know that she is firmly in charge of John's high-profile cases.

It is ironic that John's murder cases have landed in Judge Hart's court. What is more ironic is that Lindsey Moreland is the prosecuting attorney for this case. The last time I appeared in Judge Hart's courtroom, I was the defendant on trial for murder and Lindsey was the government's prosecuting attorney.

The months following John's preliminary hearing have been uneventful. The calls to the office from reporters wanting an interview have slowed down. The video clip of John blowing a kiss to the grieving parents during his preliminary hearing went viral. The clip was shown dozens of times on local and national TV. For days our phone had been swamped from reporters wanting an interview or at least a quote on what I thought about John blowing that kiss. Maria always uses her stock answer when reporters call, "No comment now or in the future." I can tell that she really enjoys shutting them down by how happy it makes her to say that before hanging up.

She is still upset with me because I took John's case against her advice. She knows that I never shied away from publicity before and it amuses her that I avoid the media in this case. Every time I dodge a reporter, she takes delight in reminding me that I'm trying to hide the fact I am representing *El Diablo*.

I have consistently visited with John all through Winter and Spring. It is late Summer now and I still dread the time I have to spend with him. As recommended, I visit him at least once a week. I always keep my visits as brief as possible. Up until now, there hasn't been any activity in his cases. His sister called this morning and made arrangements for me to meet her tomorrow night for dinner. She told Maria that she wanted to talk to me about her mother and about the case. I am surprised that she called to schedule a meeting. Dorothy and I have been in contact frequently and she never mentioned going out socially. She has become very close with Maria and they talk on the phone a lot.

John's murder cases are in the stage of waiting for the Grand Jury to indict him. There hasn't been any new developments in his case so there hasn't been much for Dorothy and I to talk about.

John has recently been indicted by the Davidson County Grand Jury for all three murders. His cases are assigned to Judge Hart's court. The Judge will set dates for motions and possibly even trial dates at our status meeting today.

I can only guess how Judge Hart will feel about me being a licensed attorney, representing a guilty client, for the second time in her courtroom.

When I was on trial for murder in front of her and representing myself, I really pushed the limits of what an attorney could get away with when representing their client.

The Judge allowed me a little latitude then because I was my own attorney. In my trial I had been both a smartass and a showboat. I know better now and I have no plans to be either.

My goal in Judge Hart's court is to make the system work the way it should. The facts and the law are in perfect alignment for John's case to be won with a Motion to Suppress. If I can make that happen, I will be able to forego the necessity and rigors of a jury trial.

For my motion to be successful, the Judge will face a difficult decision. She will have to rule that allowing Rebecca's panties into evidence for a jury to decide John's guilt or innocence would violate my client's rights to a fair trial. If the Judge rules Rebecca's panties are untrustworthy as evidence to convict John, she could dismiss all three murder charges against him. Whether dismissal would be appropriate depends on how important the evidence is to the prosecution's cases in convicting John. It is my professional opinion, and I will argue, that without the use of Rebecca's panties as evidence all the cases will fall apart and John will have to be set free.

Dismissing John's murder charges will be a tough call for Judge Hart to make. A dismissal will bring intense media scrutiny on her decision. Many judges might be tempted to rule in favor of the government and allow Rebecca's panties into evidence. It would be easier for some judges to allow the jury to decide whether or not the panties are trustworthy evidence. Judge Hart doesn't have a reputation as being that kind of judge. If I can prove to her that allowing Rebecca's panties into evidence would be unfair to my client, I know she will obey the law and dismiss the cases against him. First, I'm going to have to find Wishbone to make that happen.

It isn't only John's case that has kept me in a sour mood these last few months. Laura and I have only talked once since John's preliminary hearing when she told me she may be falling in love with me. I didn't know how to respond to her admission. My first instinct was to tell her she would be wasting her time, but I'm not in the habit of lying. She looked sad when I had told her, "I need time, I'm not ready to commit yet."

Her answer struck a chord with me, "Oh, you're ready to make a commitment to a woman. You just don't know which woman. Just remember this. If you don't make a commitment to somebody, you're going to wind up by yourself, Cowboy."

Laura's words, reminding me that I am headed for a life of loneliness, have haunted me the last few months. I haven't felt this alone since I was in jail. She only speaks to me when we are in the same courtroom or passing each other in the halls of the courthouse. She let me know that she is giving me space to let me "figure it out."

Maria has provided me with some comfort in the months since John came into our lives. She has taken on more responsibility in my law practice since I have been busy with John's case. I believe she senses that I am preoccupied with John and makes sure I stay sharp and don't let anything slip. We are like a mom and pop operation. Only she's not mom and I'm not pop.

Laura was right. Maria was in the back of my mind when I told her that I needed time and I wasn't ready to settle down. Putting my romantic life on hold made no sense then and it makes no sense now. For all I know, my infatuation with Maria is one-sided.

John's case is looking better. However, Wishbone is proving to be a difficult person to locate but we are getting closer. Dakota has integrated himself in the biker culture. He's made friends and contacts while searching for Wishbone. Dakota told me he has gained some respect for Wishbone and the biker lifestyle in his quest.

He appreciates the freedom of being on the road that the biker's lifestyle offers. He also shares the same disdain for authority that bikers have.

Dakota phoned me as I was leaving my office for my meeting with the Judge and the D.A. He told me he learned that Wishbone's given name is David Bryson. When I got to the courthouse, I stopped by the clerk's office and had a subpoena issued for David Bryson, aka Wishbone, before I made my way to the Judge's chambers.

As I enter the outer office, Lindsey is already sitting there. The secretary notices me and proceeds to usher Lindsey and me into the Judge's Chambers.

Judge Hart is sitting at her desk as we enter. She smiles broadly at us as she stands up. She steps from behind her desk and shakes our hands. She asks us to take a seat as she returns to her desk and sits down.

The Judge folds her hands in front of her as she speaks to us, "I appreciate both of you meeting me here today. We've got a tough case, not only for the court, but for the attorneys. My reason for asking the two of you here today is to set dates for any pretrial motions. Once I've dealt with all motions, I will set dates for all three cases. I know that these are high profile cases and that an enormous amount of media attention is associated with John Lester and what he is accused of doing. I watch the local TV news too. I want these cases to run smoothly without any grandstanding."

Judge Hart is looking directly at me when she warns the two of us not to grandstand in her court. I want to remind her that we aren't invited to visit her chambers, she has summoned us. I hold my tongue though. I made a vow to myself to play it cool and not be a smartass in her court.

I am not comfortable sitting in the Judge's chambers. I feel like I am in her courtroom on trial for murder again. I had forgotten how steely and piercing her eyes are and how she makes me think she can see right through me to my soul.

I want to make this meeting as short as possible. I want to pick a date to hear my Motion to Suppress and get out of her Chambers without getting myself in trouble.

With that in mind, I look at Judge Hart and tell her, "I need a date for the Court to hear my Motion to Suppress. It is my legal opinion that you will have to dismiss all three cases once you hear the proof. I need a little time to find a witness."

Lindsey's face grows taught as I speak. Judge Hart's face never wavers from her iron gaze, that unnerves me, as she speaks. "Mr. Harris, I hope you would have convincing evidence for this Judge to dismiss the charges against your client. I hope you're not grandstanding again and you have real proof to back up your claim."

The Judge's suggestion that I might be grandstanding pisses me off and I let her know it with my response, "Judge, you should know from experience that if I thought grandstanding would help me defend John Lester then I will grandstand and tell you "I'm sorry" later. I don't need theatrics to defend him. I've got solid facts for the court to hear. Please give me a court date and you can find out for yourself if I'm bullshitting this court."

I regret my words as soon as they come out of my mouth. I broke my promise to not be a smartass and keep it cool.

She fixes me with a steely gaze. She speaks in the same tone of voice she used at my murder trial six long years ago, "Mr. Harris, these cases will move forward. It's up to you to find this mystery witness. I am setting a court date of September 12th at 9:00 a.m. for your Motion to be heard. There will not be a continuance granted by this Court if you don't have your witness in court on that date to testify." She then dismisses Lindsey and me.

I am not sure if Judge Hart has given me enough time to find Wishbone. That is the only concern I have from our meeting with her. My concern that we won't find him fades away as I'm leaving the courthouse. I check my voicemail and there is a message from Dakota. His message is short and simple, "Found Wishbone. We will go see him tonight. Pick you up at midnight. Bring your gun."

CHAPTER 39

I should be totally relaxed but I'm not. It's a great evening to be outside. I'm sitting in a lawn chair. It's a pleasant late summer night and I'm outside my duplex waiting for Dakota to pick me up. I'm gazing at the street lights while pondering the situation I'm in.

Normally, I would issue a subpoena and let a process server with the Sheriff's Department serve the witness that I need for court. John Lester is not a normal client and David Bryson, aka Wishbone, is not a normal witness. First off, a process server with the Sheriff's Department would not have any luck locating this witness to serve a subpoena. Even if a process server found him, and served the subpoena, it is unlikely that he would ever obey a summons to court. Second, I need to build a relationship with Wishbone if I want him to help me. The best way to do that is to meet him and talk to him in person.

The Judge has already let me know that I will not be getting a continuance on the hearing for my Motion to Suppress if my witness doesn't show up for court. Not only do Dakota and I need to serve Wishbone the subpoena, we need to make sure he will show up and testify in court. Sitting here waiting on Dakota, I don't have any idea on how to make that happen.

Dakota has immersed himself in the biker culture. I guess something about the image of a self-sufficient loner riding across America's plains has resonated with him. He has grown to appreciate that outlaw bikers reject the laws constructed by society and adopt new rules according to their circumstances.

The contact I had with bikers, while working in the clubs,

was minimal. Bikers didn't normally hang out in the clubs where I used to work. Although I don't see eye to eye with the biker culture, I do have a healthy respect for the world of the outlaw biker. I have to because no matter what you think of bikers, the bikers I encountered, while working at Sherry's, were not playing at being badasses. In my experience, the outlaw biker life has its own rules. They have a brother-hood code and they avoid interacting with the government. Bikers utilize an old west-type justice system whenever they meet with trouble.

Dakota has discovered that hunting down Wishbone is a difficult and somewhat dangerous job. He started his search for Wishbone at Devil's Hideout, the biker bar. Tiffany, the bartender, was able to get word to Wishbone that Dakota is working for me on John's case and I need to talk to him.

While Dakota was at Devil's Hideout, Wishbone sent word through two of his Outcast brothers that he didn't need to talk to me and that I'd be better off minding my own business. The two "brothers" had introduced themselves to Dakota by their street names. One called himself Jinx and the other referred to himself as Tiny. Dakota told me that Jinx did most of the talking and was the one who passed Wishbone's message. Dakota said that it turned into a tense situation when he told them that it was my business to talk with Wishbone and that it was going to happen. It was only a matter of when and how. He said they bristled up when he told them that. He thought he was headed for a brawl with both of Wishbone's "brothers". It turned into a standoff that ended with a phone call from Jinx to Wishbone. Dakota had to stand toe to toe with Tiny while Jinx called Wishbone and then handed the phone to Dakota and said, "You want to talk to Wishbone - he's on the phone". When Dakota got on the phone, Wishbone said, "You tell this hot-shot attorney if he wants to talk, he can meet me at the Outcasts' Clubhouse tonight after midnight. That is, if he's got the balls to show up." Dakota got the club's address from Jinx and Tiny before they left.

The forty caliber Glock I'm cradling in my lap brings a

reality to the situation Dakota and I are in. I don't usually carry a gun even though I've got a carry permit. When I worked at Sherry's, I was never without a gun. I never thought I'd need to carry a gun again after I became an attorney. Here I sit waiting, in the dark for Dakota to pick me up. We are going to inject ourselves into a possible violent event. Seems like old times to me.

For the first time in years I've got butterflies. Butterflies is the twitch I would get in my stomach when I first started working at Sherry's right before a scuffle or a hostile threat would break out. Butterflies was the realization that I could get hurt. The longer I worked at Sherry's and faced violent or dangerous situations routinely, the butterflies finally vanished. Now that uneasy feeling in my stomach is back tonight.

The twitch in my stomach vanishes as Dakota pulls into my driveway. Knowing he will be with me is comforting. As I get into his car, I slide my Glock into the waistband at the back of my jeans. I pull the t-shirt I am wearing over the top of the gun to conceal it. This allows me reasonably quick access to my weapon.

As he drives, Dakota explains to me that he checked out the Outcasts' Clubhouse earlier. The clubhouse is located on Rio Vista Drive in an area of Nashville called Madison. He tells me that the clubhouse is inside a compound with an eight-foot metal fence surrounding it. The compound is set up strategically. The Cumberland River makes a natural barrier across the back. It has large open fields with metal fencing surrounding the rest of the compound. All of this makes it impossible for anyone to approach the bikers' clubhouse without being observed. The driveway to the compound is about thirty yards off the road with a large parking lot in front where there's a gate.

As Dakota and I proceed down the driveway, the only thing we can see is the street light illuminating the inside of the compound. I am struck by the thought that once we were behind the gate no one would ever be any the wiser as to what happens to us after we had entered. Nevertheless, here we are. As we pull into the parking lot and get out of the car, the two Outcasts' that Dakota confronted earlier, Jinx and Tiny, are standing at the entrance in front of the gate. Jinx is the first to speak, as we walk up. He tells Dakota, "You must be the stupidest son-of-a-bitch I've ever seen, coming out here like this."

I hear Jinx's words and cringe. He is deliberately making it testy for Dakota. I'm not sure how Dakota will reply. We both know that we need to play it cool. At the same time, it is important that we stand our ground if we want respect. Dakota's response to Jinx does both of these things when he says, "We're going to get along a whole lot better if you stop calling me names."

Well here we are, with Dakota's response, this situation may get violent. I tense up and start planning my next move if either Jinx or Tiny display any hostile intent.

Luck is with us, Jinx shakes his head when he hears Dakota's smartass response and says, "Can't say you're not stupid, but you've got the balls of a bank robber, I'll have to give you that. If you're packing, leave your hardware here and I'll take the two of you back to meet Wishbone."

"That's not going to happen", I announce with a stern voice. It is the first time Jinx and Tiny hear me speak. Both of them act surprised. My statement breaks the relaxed atmosphere created by the exchange between Dakota and Jinx. The tension has eased somewhat. I have fucked that up with my refusal to give up our weapons. I don't care, Dakota and I are not going through that gate unarmed.

It is obvious that Jinx takes exception to my refusal to relinquish our guns. Jinx lets me know exactly how he feels by standing up straight and squaring his shoulders aggressively as he tells me, "Then you're not coming in and you can take your sorry asses and leave right now if you know what's good for you."

Before I can reply, Dakota steps in front of Jinx. They are face to face, not twelve inches apart, with Dakota staring at Jinx. Dakota has a deadly look on his face that let us all know that, depending on what happens next, we are on the edge of some serious shit. Dakota doesn't even raise his voice, he simply says, "I warned you about calling us names. Now it looks like we're never going to be friends."

Things are getting out of hand fast. Dakota wants trouble and Jinx shows no interest in backing off. I have to get control of this dilemma we are in or face the real prospect of bloodletting being unleashed at the front gate of the compound. Before Jinx can answer Dakota's challenge, I quickly step between them and speak directly to Jinx, "Everybody cool it. No reason for this to get out of hand. You voiced your opinion that you thought Dakota was stupid for coming here when we first arrived. Well Dakota's not stupid and neither am I. Only a stupid man would be here like this without a gun. And only a stupid man would go in there without a gun. You can tell Wishbone that I've got a legitimate reason for being here. I've got a subpoena with his name on it and we're not going to leave until he talks to me."

Jinx steps back, takes a long hard look at Dakota as he speaks to me and says, "Ok legal eagle, you and your friend stay here. Tiny will keep you company. I'll give your tidings to Wishbone. You might not like the answer you get."

Jinx turns to go through the gate leaving Dakota and I facing Tiny, who is standing between us and the front gate. The time waiting there with Tiny turns into an awkward twenty minutes. The name "Tiny" is a misnomer, Tiny is probably one of the biggest men I have ever seen. No one speaks until Jinx returns.

Jinx whispers in Tiny's ear before he turns to face us. I can't help but notice that Jinx has the handle of a revolver sticking out of the waistband of his pants that wasn't there before.

"Follow me", Jinx says while staring at Dakota with a vicious look in his eyes. Jinx is a small wiry guy and he seems to have that complex most small men have about starting trouble. It is obvious to me that Jinx and Dakota are itching to get at each other. I need to get a handle on their animosity or this is never going to work.

We follow Jinx and Tiny through the gate into the compound. As I glance over the inside of the compound, I see that there are two buildings in the enclosure. The first building we pass is the club's motorcycle garage. It houses bikes in different stages of repair. The other building is the clubhouse. It has picnic tables sitting off to the side in a patio-type area.

Dakota and I follow the two bikers into the clubhouse. The inside of the clubhouse is dimly lit. There is a bar in the back, a juke box in the corner and tables sitting out away from the bar. The club is empty except for three bikers sitting at one of the tables in the back of the club. Jinx takes us back to the table where the three bikers are sitting.

Jinx walks around the table and stands behind the biker sitting at the end of the table, looks at him and says, "Here they are Wishbone. What do you want to do with them?"

I have Jinx pegged as the agitator. Jinx is looking to start trouble and Dakota is looking to accommodate him. If possible, I need to mollify the rift between Jinx and Dakota if I am to have any chance of preventing a free for all from ensuing.

I take a quick survey of the room. There are a total of five bikers in the room. Wishbone is sitting at the end of the table facing us. Jinx is strategically standing behind Wishbone's right shoulder. The other two are sitting at the table with Wishbone, one on his right and the other on his left. That leaves Tiny standing next to my left shoulder and Dakota by my right shoulder.

Jinx is the one to keep an eye on because he is the one who has the quickest access to a weapon and he is spoiling for a confrontation.

I think it will be wise for me to start a dialogue with Wishbone immediately. Hopefully, with Wishbone and I conversing, Jinx and Dakota will cool it. I look directly at Wishbone before he can speak and say, "We're here and we're not leaving until I talk to you about what you know was going on at John Lester's house the last time you were there. I know you were there; I can prove that. I'm also doing you a favor by coming here to talk to you. It could have been Detective Fowler, the lead detective handling John's case, snooping around asking questions instead of Dakota and me. You can choose not to talk to me and I promise you the police will be in touch with you soon."

Before Wishbone can answer, Jinx chimes in with, "I think you're a lying shyster and that you and your buddy need to get your asses out of here while you still can"

Jinx has called me a Shyster. Now I am pissed. I decide to ignore Jinx's insult and speak directly to Wishbone, "I'd advise you tell your boy standing behind you that I don't lie and I don't back off."

Without waiting for Wishbone to reply, Jinx screams, "I'll teach you to call me boy!" I see him reaching for the revolver in his front waistband.

As Jinx reaches for the gun in his waistband, I quickly stepped back leaving Tiny still standing on my left shoulder but slightly in front of me. I reach behind my back and put my hand on the handle of my Glock to draw it so I can shoot Jinx if necessary. Before either Jinx or I have time to pull our weapons, Dakota has his pistol in his hand and pointed directly at Jinx's head ready to pull the trigger.

I yell at the top of my voice, "Everybody freeze and no one gets hurt!" My outburst seems to work. Everyone stays in place with Dakota covering Jinx. Wishbone and his two buddies are still seated at the table and Tiny doesn't move from his position in front of me.

I speak as calmly as I can and loud enough to make sure everyone in the room can hear me, "There is no need to take the predicament we all are in to the next level. Everyone in the room is smart enough to know that if this situation escalates, it won't end tonight. I don't think anybody wants that."

I want everybody in the room to cool off but that isn't going to happen until Dakota lowers his weapon. I look towards Dakota and say, "Lower your weapon, nobody's going to die tonight."

Dakota's response is what is needed to curtail the stress everyone is experiencing when he says, "No can do. I will lower my weapon when Jinx takes his hand off the handle of his revolver. He and I need to come to an agreement that if he calls either of us any more names, we're gonna put the guns down and Jinx and I are gonna duke it out."

Dakota's declaration, challenging Jinx, is perfect for alleviating the intense pressure of the situation. Dakota calling Jinx out is a good-humored way of letting Jinx, and his brothers, know that they have our respect and at the same time that we are demanding their respect. Dakota's use of humor allows everyone involved to ratchet back this situation somewhat and save face at the same time.

Wishbone speaks for the first time, "Jinx take your paw off your weapon." Jinx does, which prompts Dakota to lower his gun.

Wishbone is a surprise, he doesn't look so much like a biker, as an ex-Navy Seal. He is muscled up with tattoos everywhere that I can see. He has close cropped hair with a beard and mustache.

Wishbone looks at me and says, "Ok Mr. Harris, you've got my attention. What do you want to know about John Lester? Before you answer, you should know how I feel about the sick bastard. If he killed those girls, I don't want to help him and if I get the chance, I will kill the slime ball myself."

It is no stretch of anyone's imagination to understand why Wishbone feels that way about killing John. I also notice the little nuance that he referred to me as Mr. Harris. That is Wishbone showing me respect. It is important that I show him the same respect if I am to have any chance of getting his help.

"Just call me William please and I would appreciate it if you didn't abbreviate my name and substitute Bill instead." Then I add, "You wouldn't be helping John, you would be helping me."

Wishbone leans back with a curious look on his face and asks me. "Why would I want to help you, William?"

"Good question. It strikes me that an outfit like yours needs a good attorney from time to time." I reply.

Wishbone chuckles and asks, "Are you a good attorney?"

"Damn sure am. I've won my last two murder trials. Plus, only a good attorney would put himself and his best friend in the position I find myself in tonight to help a client he fucking hates. The good thing is I don't hate you or your brothers and I know you could use my help." I answer.

Wishbone doesn't respond immediately; he seems like he is thinking over the proposal I made before he gives me a response. "OK, we got a deal. You'll be the club's attorney and I'll testify for you."

"Great. You also need to know that I won't help you break the law but if you do break the law, I'll do my best to help you avoid the consequences. If you can agree to that then we have a deal." I tell him.

Wishbone's reply is short and to the point, "Deal." Then he asks me, "What do you need to know about the night before John Lester was arrested?"

"I only have a few questions I would ask you to truthfully testify to. If your answer is yes to my questions then you are my witness. Is that agreed to?"

Wishbone gives me another short reply which is straight to the point, "You got it."

Now we are getting somewhere, Wishbone isn't wasting my time and I'm not wasting his. With that in mind, I combine all the things I need answers to into three quick questions. "Did Bobby Meyers leave a pair of panties at John Lester's house the night you were there? Did John Lester smack Bobby Meyers that same night? Did Bobby Meyers tell John he would get even with him that night?" I ask Wishbone.

Wishbone answers, "It looks like you've got yourself a witness and the club has a new attorney. I think we are going to know each other for a long time."

Before Dakota and I leave the clubhouse, we make arrangements to stay in touch with Wishbone. Neither Dakota nor I speak a word as we exit the gate leaving the club house compound to go to the car.

Both of us sit in the car, staring out into space, without

speaking until Dakota finally says to me, "You are full of shit. What do you mean by you don't lie and you don't back off? By the way, I'm going to need a fucking raise."

CHAPTER 40

*I*t was the first day I have taken off since becoming John's lawyer. I spent most of this day sleeping.

Dakota drove me home after we left the Outcasts' club last night and we sat in the back yard of my duplex talking. We were too keyed up to go to sleep.

Dakota left my house about the same time the sun was peeking up over the horizon. I called Maria to let her know I wasn't coming into the office today and for her to take care of things. I didn't tell her what happened last night. I knew she would be pissed when she found out I'd done something so stupid. I decided to take my ass chewing later and sleep in.

Tonight, I'm meeting Dorothy Lester for dinner. She has chosen to meet at Jimmy Kelly's, one of the oldest restaurants in Nashville.

Dorothy had called me and stopped by the office several times since her brother's preliminary hearing. She was friendly and warm and I enjoy talking to her. Dorothy and Maria have become fond of each other.

The times Dorothy and I have been in each other's presence in the last few months she has always been business like and never flirtatious. That's why I find it strange that she has asked me to meet her for dinner. She chose one of the swankiest restaurants in town to dine. Dinner at this restaurant is expensive and not necessarily a business-like atmosphere.

If she is thinking about taking our relationship to something more than a business relationship, I find the idea of having an affair with Dorothy intriguing. Of course, I would have to tell her that anything between us would have to wait until long after her brother's trial is finished.

Still, I am feeling pretty good about myself as the maître d' leads me to the back of the restaurant. The building used to be a doctor's house that was built over a hundred years ago. It is something to see and, in its prime, had been a seven-bedroom home on the outskirts of downtown Nashville. The décor is fancy and I can see Dorothy sitting at a table for four. There is another woman sitting beside her.

Dorothy stands up and smiles as I approached. She shakes my hand, hugs me and says, "I want you to meet my life partner, Karen Montgomery."

I sure didn't see that coming. Now I am more confused than ever about what Dorothy's intentions are for inviting me here tonight. It's obvious this isn't a date and there won't be any future affair.

Karen stands up, shakes my hand, lightly smiles and says, "William, I am so glad to meet you finally. Dorothy has told me so much about you. If what she tells me is accurate, you are one the most interesting men I might ever meet."

She is about my height with shoulder length auburn hair and the greenest eyes I've ever seen. I can see what Dorothy sees in Karen - she is gorgeous.

I am looking at Karen, but speaking to Dorothy, when I say, "That's intriguing and nice of you to say Karen. But I don't know how Dorothy could know enough about me to make you think I could be one of the most interesting people you might meet."

"I can answer that." Dorothy says, "I have several reasons for inviting you here tonight. First, because I like you and I want you to meet Karen. I want her to know and meet the people I like and trust. Also, I want to talk to you about your reasons for avoiding the press. But most of all, I've got a confession to make. When I first hired you, I also hired private investigators to check out everything about you, William Harris. Don't be offended. I had no reason to think you were not on the level. I've learned that it's a good business practice to know as much as I can about an individual that I'm doing business with."

"What I've learned about you is that you are an enigmatic man. My investigators found out all kinds of interesting things about you. You weren't a very good college football player, but you did make decent grades. I even know that you lived with a call-girl for a couple of years while you were in law school. All of that was interesting. But the most significant thing I found out about you is that you were tried and found not guilty for killing someone. I read the summary of your murder case and I know you killed Jack Adams because you were protecting a police officer. That's what you do, you protect people who deserve it."

The reports of people who knew you before you went to law school helped me come to the same conclusion. Everyone my investigators spoke to about you said the same things. You can be trusted. You're a straight shooter and you will take care of any trouble that starts. In short William, you take care and protect." She said all this to me and it took me by surprise.

Dorothy went on, "You make me feel safe. You made my mother and I feel secure at John's preliminary hearing when you shielded us from the media and that poor girl's parents. You're such a paradox. You can be very violent and very gentle. After the hearing, when Rebecca Springer's father attacked us in the parking garage, I never felt one ounce of fear. I knew you would protect us. You also protected that poor girl's father. You didn't hit him back and you didn't call the police to have him arrested for assaulting you."

Dorothy looks at me across the table and says, "That is why we don't understand what you're doing William. Why are you protecting my brother? You know he doesn't deserve it. You know he's guilty."

I take a minute to gather my thoughts before answering her.

"First off, I didn't "live" with a call-girl. Anna was a room-mate and a friend. Our relationship was strictly platonic. That's all I'm going to say on that subject." I say this with a shrug and a smile.

Before either Dorothy or Karen can speak, I quickly add, "I'm not protecting John. I'm protecting the system. I don't believe the government has a case it should win. My belief is based on facts and law. If the facts in his case are presented in a proper and legal manner, there is a good chance that the law will set your brother free. My job is to make sure the system works. If the government doesn't have a case it can successfully prosecute, your brother should be set free. It's as simple as that."

Karen, who has been listening intently, says, "Dorothy told me you would do what is necessary to free John, if you could do it within the bounds of the law because that is your duty. But we're bewildered and surprised that you haven't made any statements to the media in his case."

As I listen to Karen talk, it immediately becomes clear to me that they have a close bond and Karen is an equal partner in their relationship.

Before I can answer, Dorothy speaks up, "Yes William, you've never been shy addressing the media in any of your other cases. You were basically a media hound. Why now? Is it because you don't want the public to associate you with El Diablo?"

I have to smile when I hear Dorothy refer to her brother using the Spanish translation for The Devil. I know she has been talking to Maria. I am surprised that the two of them are familiar enough with each other for Maria to let Dorothy know that she thinks of Dorothy's brother as The Devil.

I simply say, "You've been talking to Maria, haven't you? She is not timid when it comes to expressing her opinion."

Dorothy quickly adds, "You're right about that. Maria is not bashful when it comes to talking about you. She really cares for you. I hope you appreciate that."

My response is a little curt but to the point, "I do appreciate Maria. She's efficient and has a great rapport with my clients. She is everything a lawyer could want for their legal assistant."

Dorothy looks at me with a twinkle in her eyes and says,

"I'm not talking about a good secretary that dotes after her boss. I'm talking about a woman who cares for her man. I'm talking about a man, you William Harris, who gets cold feet and refuses to make a commitment or admit he cares for a woman."

As I listen to Dorothy express her thoughts about me and Maria, Karen places her hand over Dorothy's while smiling. The conversation has gone far astray from any legal issues concerning John. Before I have a chance to give a response to Dorothy's account of my relationship with Maria and what her expectations of that relationship are, the server comes and takes our order. We spend the rest of the evening enjoying dinner and getting to know each other. It is easy to tell that Dorothy and Karen are in love. They explain to me that the only reason they have not married yet is that Dorothy's mother would not approve.

As dinner comes to a close, Karen looks at me and asks, "William, would you be willing to reconsider your position of not speaking to the media?"

"I really prefer not to talk to the media and hope you understand.", is my quick answer.

Karen, speaking for the two of them, says, "Yes, we do understand but it would mean so much to Dorothy's mother. We would like for you to make a comment expressing how sorry the family is for the deaths of those three innocent little girls. Could you do that if you were paid extra?"

"How much extra?" I ask.

"Would $10,000.00 be enough?", Karen asks, "Make it $25,000.00 and you've got a deal", I reply.

Karen's response is quick, "Great, we will have a courier deliver a check to your office tomorrow."

I responded, "That's fine but would you make the check out to Dakota Gray please and send it to his address? I know you have his address since I'm sure you've had your investigators check him out as well. Oh, and please don't tell Maria about it in your little conversations. I won't lie to her but I'd rather she not find out that I gave up that much money before I figure out how to explain it to her."

Both of the women look perplexed. Dorothy is the first one to speak, "Dakota Gray is your private investigator. That seems like a lot of money for those services."

I reply, "Let's just say Dakota earned every penny last night."

As we are leaving the restaurant, Dorothy tells me, "I know you're gonna win this case William. That's what you do, you win. I should be scared that my brother is going to be released but I'm not. That's also because of you. I know that you will figure out a way to protect us."

CHAPTER 41

*T*he days following my meeting with Judge Hart and Assistant District Attorney Lindsay Moreland have gone by slowly. It strikes me as I am sitting here at CCA, waiting for what I hope will be my last visit with John, that I have been his attorney for all four seasons now.

It is September and the weather is perfect. Normally, weather like this makes me cheerful and glad I'm alive, and most importantly, not in jail. For the most part I have been depressed every day waiting for John's hearing tomorrow. I am dreading it. I know that no matter how much I don't want to go through the hearing to suppress the panties, I have to do what is necessary.

Tomorrow morning, 9 o'clock sharp, is when Judge Hart has scheduled the hearing for my Motion. Everything is in place for my client to receive a successful ruling from the court. My witnesses are lined up to testify. I always knew Larry Hargrove would be in court to testify for John. It's good to know that Wishbone will also show up.

Wishbone lost no time in taking me up on my offer to be the Outcasts' attorney. I am representing three members of the Outcasts for assault charges. The Leader of the biker gang is not shy about calling me seeking my advice on hypothetical questions. His questions to me are about what could happen if a certain law is broken and what the possible consequences might be.

Based on mutual respect, he and I have developed a strong bond in the months following our near melee at the Outcasts' club. He trusts me and I am certain he will be in court tomorrow.

I have thoroughly prepared both Wishbone and Larry for their testimony. I'm certain their testimony will be truthful. I have also instructed Wishbone when to take the fifth while he is testifying. I feel like John's defense to his murder charges will work.

Winning has always been a natural high for me. I am certain that I am going to win tomorrow. Usually, I would be in a great mood to win a murder case but not this time.

Knowing that I am going to win is the source of my melancholy. I know what winning his case means and I'm afraid of what I will have to do.

Maria, as usual, has kept my spirits at an even keel. She has been a source of comfort for me these last few months. Today, she seemed more attentive to me than usual. As the day ended and I was leaving the office to go see John, she gave me a hug, with a twinkle in her eyes, and said, "It's going to be alright, I promise."

"How can you know that?" I asked her.

"Because it's you William. You will figure a way to make it right. That's why I know it's going to be alright." She said and hugged me even tighter.

At that moment, I was tempted to kiss her. I think she was expecting me to kiss her, but I resisted, knowing I still wasn't ready to go there yet. If something happens between me and Maria, I know it will be all or nothing.

Instead, I gently broke away from her arms, while I kissed her lightly on her forehead and said, "Thanks, but I'm not so sure everything will be alright this time."

Before leaving the office, I told Maria good night and that I would see her tomorrow after the hearing.

The sound of metal on metal of the doors opening, allowing John into the visitation area, reminds me of where I am and my main purpose for being there today.

I have faithfully visited John while he has been in jail,

keeping him informed of his case. He knows that Larry and Wishbone will testify in his defense. He knows there is a good chance Judge Hart will grant my motion to disallow Rebecca Springers' panties into evidence. He is well aware that, if I am successful, then the state's case will fall apart and he will go scott free.

What John doesn't know, but will as soon as we talk, is that he is not going to taunt the parents of those little girls again.

That is my primary thought, as John walks across the floor to meet me. He still has that shit-eating grin on his face as he sits down across from me at the visitation table. He doesn't know it yet, but he is about to drop that grin.

As usual, I don't stand up to greet him nor do I offer him a handshake.

I want to get right to the point and get out of here as soon as possible, so I say, "John, I didn't see you blow that kiss at the parents the last time we were in court. But you better believe that you will not do anything like that tomorrow. We are going to come to that understanding right now. If we don't come to an understanding, then I can guarantee you that you are not going to like the results."

CHAPTER 42

*J*ohn listens to William but thinks he is bluffing; besides he has been looking forward to fucking with those little whores' parents for months. Just remembering the looks on their faces when he blew them a kiss makes him smile.

"Counselor, who are you trying to kid. You wouldn't do anything to me for merely blowing a kiss, now would you?" He asks.

CHAPTER 43

"Yes, I would." I reply and grab him by the back of his neck and pull him to me until his forehead is touching mine.

"You are going to get off tomorrow. I'm sure that you want to go on living a peaceful life after that. If you do want to live, it would be in your best interests to sit in court tomorrow, mind your own fucking business and leave the parents of those children alone. If you don't, I promise you I will kill you. I will break my oath to the law. I will hunt you down after you're free. I will be your worst nightmare. What's more, I don't believe a jury would convict me for killing you. The last time I killed someone, a jury let me off because I had to kill. I believe a jury would let me off again because you need killing – you sorry sack of shit."

CHAPTER 44

*J*ohn is terrified. He knows this man isn't bluffing. He is certain that if he doesn't behave in court tomorrow, William will kill him. He will go to that dark place beyond death that petrifies him. But he needs some reassurance that William won't kill him anyway if he does act right. He needs to hear William promise he won't kill him. John needs to use William's honesty against him.

"How do I know you won't kill me anyway? How can I trust you?" John asks.

CHAPTER 45

"*F*air enough," I reply, "you leave those parents alone tomorrow and I promise you that you will go free and you will never have to look over your shoulder worrying about me. Do we have a deal?"

CHAPTER 46

*J*ohn is starting to relax now. He has William's promise. All John has to do is be good in court tomorrow. Then he will be free and he won't have to worry about William. It is an easy deal to make.

"We've got a deal.", John says as William lets him go and leaves the visiting gallery.

CHAPTER 47

*T*he drive home to my duplex in Donelson went by fast. I am leaving the jail just as the sun is going down. It is perfect T-shirt weather. The beautiful weather is exactly what I need. I've been focused on John's case constantly. I am going to sit in a lawn chair in the backyard by myself. For most of my life, I have been alone and it has never bothered me. After my encounter with John today and knowing what I have to do, it strikes me that a little company tonight wouldn't be the worst thing in the world.

My thoughts are interrupted as I turn in my driveway and see, in the glow of my headlights, Maria's car parked there. Maria is sitting on the porch to the side entrance of my place.

My headlights also catch Maria when she stands up as I turn into the driveway. She is wearing the same white dress she had on at the office today. The headlights reflecting on her show the faint outline of her hips and legs through the dress.

As she stands by the porch and waits for me to approach, I can't help thinking how beautiful she is. The wind is softly blowing her long black hair over her shoulders and across her dark eyes. Maria smiles at me as I move closer to her. I have never desired or needed a woman as much as I need Maria right now. Thoughts of wanting to be alone flee my mind completely.

I have a quizzical look on my face as I ask her "What are you doing here?"

She answers, "I'm here because you need me tonight. I'm here because I will always be there for you when you need me.

I'm here because I'm not going to let you be alone tonight. I love you William Harris. I will always love you. I know you love me too, even if you won't admit it. I'm staying tonight because I'm not going to let you be alone when you need me the most. Besides that, you forgot to do something before you left the office today."

I close my eyes while listening to everything she says. She is right, I am in love with her. It's time. I've wanted Maria from almost the first day we met. I'd let myself fall in love with a woman for the first time in my life.

She and I are standing close. We are face to face as I put my hands on her shoulders, look into her eyes and say, "I love you too. I don't only want you for tonight. I want and need you for all of eternity. I want to take care of you and protect you. That is my commitment to you." I whisper and pause before I asked her, "What did I forget to do at the office today?"

Maria is smiling, with tears of joy in her eyes, as she answers, "You forgot to kiss me, you big Cabron."

I like the way she calls me dumbass in Spanish. It's sounds sexy when she says it.

CHAPTER 48

*M*y ride on the elevator at the courthouse finds me thinking about last night. I should be concentrating on John's hearing. My Motion to Suppress Rebecca Springer's panties is scheduled to be heard in front of Judge Hart in less than an hour. Instead, I can't stop thinking about last night with Maria.

For the first time since I had taken this case, I woke up in a great mood. Waking up next to Maria is a commitment that I'm not going to have any trouble keeping. My memories of making love to her last night would get me through the tough day ahead. It isn't the first time I made love to a woman knowing it isn't just a fleeting moment of passion, but I always knew before that any such passionate moments had no chance of enduring.

Making love with Maria last night had been a slow and sensual affair. We'd gone straight to my bedroom as soon as we entered the house. When we got there, we slowly undressed each other. She insisted that I leave the lights on, she said, "I want you to see me naked." After we reached our height of passion, I lay on my back exhausted while Maria cuddled on my chest. She laid her head on my shoulder and had her arm across my waist as we talked. I explained to her what had to be done in John's case. She told me she understood and that she supports me.

She said, "I'm your woman now and you're my man. We will always be there for each other. I will support you no matter what."

I plan to keep the memories of our night together with me throughout the day. It doesn't matter that I am not thinking about John's case right now. I have the case well prepared.

Wishbone and Larry Hargrove have been prepped and are ready to testify. I know that both the facts and the law are in my favor. Unfortunately, because of those facts and law, John's case is going to work out in his favor.

Knowing that Maria will be there for me when John's hearing is done puts a smile on my face. A smile I quickly lose as the elevator doors open and I step out. The hall is crammed with reporters scrambling to get a quote for the evening news. Once they see that it is John's attorney getting off the elevator, I am swarmed.

The reporters are all pointing their cameras in my face while barking questions at me. My obligation to Dorothy necessitates that I interact with the reporters on her family's behalf. They stand around me in a semi-circle.

I take the first question from a female reporter who is directly in front of me, she asks, "Is John Lester going to blow a kiss to the victims' parents today?"

I reply, "I spoke to Mr. Lester yesterday and I can tell you that he deeply regrets his actions the last time we were in court. He has assured me that there will not be a repeat of that type of behavior today."

The reporter quickly hits me with a follow-up question, "Mr. Harris, how can you assure the parents that Mr. Lester will not repeat the same despicable performance?"

It's a fair question. The video of John blowing a kiss to the parents of the girls had surfaced again on TV as we approached today's hearing. The speculation about whether or not the sadistic asshole will antagonize the parents in court today is a hot topic in the media. The reporter asking the question has no way of knowing what I know. If she had been in my meeting with John yesterday, she would know that he would not cause any problems today. She would have seen the fear in John's eyes when I told him that I would kill him if he did anything to add to the suffering of the parents. She would know that he had no intention of calling me out on that threat.

So, with a tiny smile, I answer her, "Let me say this; I was looking straight in John's eyes yesterday and he promised me that he will not be making any gestures today. I am certain Mr. Lester will honor his promise."

The remaining reporters are all trying to get their follow-up questions about the case and my client.

I feel like I need to cut my time with the reporters short. I give the generic answer that Dorothy and I have crafted, when I say, "Mr. Lester's family is extremely sorrowful about what happened to the children. His family's prayers are with the parents, families and friends of the girls. His family is looking forward to the judicial system providing closure for all."

I nudge my way through the crowd towards the courtroom.

As I exit the crowd of reporters, I see Larry and Wishbone standing at the entrance to the courtroom. About fifteen feet from where the two of them are standing is Dorothy, Karen and Mrs. Lester. The ladies are standing with their backs to the wall looking towards me. I motion to Wishbone and Larry to wait for me in the courtroom as I ease over to the family.

Dorothy and Karen greet me with smiles and hugs. Mrs. Lester, who looks frightened and confused, asks me, "Mr. Harris I've been praying for this day. Please tell me everything is going to be ok?"

Her question shocks me back to reality. I am confident that she would be ecstatic if I told her that I thought Judge Hart would rule in our favor. The truth is that John is more than likely going to be set free. That's the reality I have been living with for some time now. It doesn't matter how assured I am, I need to temper my response to John's mom in the event the Judge rules in the government's favor. I don't want to build up her expectations only to see her hopes crushed.

I look at her while speaking gently and say, "It looks good. We'll have to wait and see what the day brings us."

My answer puts a slight smile on her face as I direct the three of them into the courtroom.

It is my first time back in Judge Hart's courtroom since

my own murder trial two years ago. Although I have been practicing law and have been in and out of this courthouse, I have never had occasion to return to this courtroom. Up until now, I have never had a client whose case wound up in front of this Judge. Being here makes me uneasy and I have an eerie feeling of dread. I don't know if it's from the memories of my trial or if I am dreading John's hearing.

I make my way to the front of the courtroom. I have to go through a gate that separates the gallery, where the spectators sit, from the official business end of the courtroom. I can see Lindsey Moreland standing alongside Detective Fowler at the table reserved for the prosecution.

When Lindsey catches my eye, she motions for me to come over to where she and Randy are standing. The three of us exchange greetings. They both have concerned looks on their faces.

Lindsey says to me, "William, Randy and I have talked to the parents of the victims and we want to make you an offer to settle Mr. Lester's cases."

I listen to what she tells me. I have a pretty good idea why she might be wanting to make me an offer, she is afraid of losing this case.

"I believe I know why you are making me an offer before we get started today. I'm pretty sure the unknown DNA on Rebecca's panties matches an individual whose name is Bobby Meyers. I'm willing to bet you that the warrant Randy served on Bobby Meyers' apartment yielded a collection of little girls' panties." I tell them. Still, the rules require that I at least listen to her offer and make sure John understands there is an offer on the table. "I'm listening. What is the government's offer?"

Lindsey takes a deep breath before she speaks, "We will take the death penalty off the table if your client pleads guilty to all three murders. He would receive a life sentence with no possibility of parole. He has to take the offer today or it's withdrawn."

Then she adds, "You know he's guilty. Convince your client to take the deal and we'll all be better off."

I reply, "You're right, I know John's guilty but I also know the government can't prove that he's guilty."

Randy, who has remained silent while listening to Lindsey and I talk, speaks up, "We all know John is guilty. You can bet your bottom dollar, with no fear of losing, that John Lester will kill again if he leaves here today a free man. That's why he needs to take the deal. You need to make it happen, William. I know you. You saved a brother officer and my best friend's life, even though it could have cost you your freedom. You did that because it was the right thing to do and that meant you had to do it. Do the right thing now and convince him to take the deal."

Before I can answer Randy, the clerk announces for all to stand, as Judge Hart takes the bench.

After everyone has taken a seat, Lindsey stands and asks Judge Hart, "Your Honor, the State has conveyed an offer of settlement in John Lester's case and both parties would request a brief recess this morning while Mr. Harris discusses the offer with the Defendant."

The District Attorney's request causes a buzz of conversation from the curiosity seekers and the reporters packed in the gallery. The Judge bangs her gavel and orders the room to quiet down. The room immediately goes quiet.

Judge Hart looks at me and says, "Mr. Harris, this Court is in recess for thirty minutes to allow you to speak with your client."

CHAPTER 49

*J*ohn is still terrified sitting in the holding cell right off the courtroom by himself. He can't shake the terror that spread over him when he met with William yesterday. He believed his attorney when he said he would kill John if he fucks with those little whores' parents again. John is sure of one thing; he isn't even going to look at the girls' parents. That hadn't been his original plan though.

Since the last hearing, he had been reliving the look on the faces of the parents when he blew them that kiss. It makes John ecstatic knowing that he has added to their misery. He has been looking forward to heightening their misery again today but he knows better after his talk with his attorney.

He knows that intensifying the parents' misery is not necessary to his defense. It is just fun. He knows he can skip the fun today and concentrate on what is important to him; being set free so he can kill again. It doesn't matter how much William terrifies him, all he has to do is sit back and let his attorney do his job and he will be free to kill again. He knows that choosing William as his attorney had been the right move. He's not sure if another attorney would have been able to get Wishbone to testify, but William has. He has John's case right where it needs to be.

CHAPTER 50

*T*he District Attorney's offer to settle John's case is what I had hoped for when I first accepted this case. If John took the deal, then a guilty man will be in prison for the rest of his life and I will have earned my money. The problem with him taking the deal is that there isn't much reason to do so. I know that Lindsey offering a deal that will spare my client's life is because she thinks the Judge will rule in our favor today. I think so too and I have to tell John that.

I follow the guard to the holding cell where my client is waiting. Normally, the cell would be packed with other prisoners waiting their turn to be seen by the Judge. Today, however, John is the only one sitting in the holding cell. Judge Hart wants no other distractions for the guards. She wants all eyes on John for security concerns.

As the guard opens the door and I enter the holding cell, he closes the door behind me, leaving me alone with John. He is sitting on the long steel bench by himself. He's lost that shit-eating grin that always pisses me off and he looks bewildered as I begin to speak to him.

"The government has offered you a deal that will save your life if you take it. You would spend the rest of your life in prison with no possibility of parole."

CHAPTER 51

*W*hen John first sees William enter the door to the holding cell, it frightens him. He didn't expect to see his attorney before court. He knows William despises him and wouldn't be here unless something was wrong. It could be that William is here to warn him once again to leave the parents alone. John is relieved to discover that the government has made an offer to settle. It calms him down now that he knows William isn't here to terrify him. He had no intention of fucking with the parents of the little bitches today.

Once John settles down and is able to think, it is clear to him that the only reason he is being offered a deal means that he has won. He has gotten away with killing the little sluts. He will be free soon. There is no reason for him to take a deal.

He finds himself in a jubilant mood for a couple of reasons. First, he is relieved to discover William isn't here to fuck with him. Second, he is certain now that he is going to be free. All he needs to do is sit back and let his attorney do his job and he will be free to kill... again.

John can't hide his satisfaction with the present turn of events and has a grin on his face when he asks sarcastically, "You see any reason that I would want to take the deal, counselor?"

CHAPTER 52

*M*y answer to John's question is swift and decisive. There won't be a counter reaction from John.

I grab him by the front of his jumpsuit, snatch him up from where he is sitting until his face is only inches from mine, and say, "You should take the deal because it makes sure a miserable fuck like you spends the rest of his life in prison."

I can smell the fear on John and he has lost that shit-eating grin as I release him from my grasp.

There is nothing further to discuss with the bastard. I alert the guard that I'm ready to return to court.

As I enter the courtroom, I glance at Lindsey and mouth the words, "No deal."

She grimaces and nods her head indicating that she understands.

CHAPTER 53

The clerk announces that Judge Hart is returning to the bench as we all stand waiting for her to sit. The guards bring John into the courtroom, where he takes a seat next to me at the Defense table, facing the Judge.

Judge Hart looks at me and asks, "Does Mr. Lester wish to enter a plea deal or do you want to proceed with your Motion to Suppress, Mr. Harris?"

I stand up to address Judge Hart, "We wish to go forward with our Motion to Suppress Your Honor," I quickly say, then take my seat.

My announcement causes another buzz from the gallery which the Judge quiets by banging her gavel.

She looks at me and says, "Mr. Harris, it's your motion. Call your first witness please."

My first two witnesses, David Bryson aka Wishbone and Larry Hargrove, testify no differently than they had when I talked to them in preparation for their testimony.

Wishbone takes the Fifth when I ask him what he was doing at John's house the night before Detective Fowler found Rebecca's panties there. After taking the Fifth on that question, Wishbone testifies truthfully that Bobby Meyers was also at John's house, along with Larry Hargrove, the night in question. Wishbone's testimony confirms that John had assaulted Bobby that night and that Bobby made the statement to John that he would "get even with John" for hitting him. Wishbone testifies that after John hit Bobby, Bobby left John's house, at which time there was only Wishbone, John and Larry remaining. Before

Michie Gibson

Bobby returned to John's house, Larry Hargrove and John left. At that time Wishbone was left there alone sitting on John's sofa.

I know the answer to my next questions for Wishbone will be pivotal in John's defense. I raise the tone of my voice to dramatize my questions and Wishbone's answers for maximum effect, in order to make my point.

"Mr. Bryson, did Bobby Meyers return to John's house before you left that night?"

David Bryson aka Wishbone replies, "Yes".

I then ask, "Did Bobby Meyers then leave before you did?"

Again, Wishbone states, "Yes."

My next question for Wishbone will be my last, his answer will more than likely set John free.

"Mr. Bryson, did Bobby Meyers have anything with him and did he say anything before he left that last time?"

Wishbone answers me loudly, letting everyone sitting in the room hear his answer. "Yes sir, Bobby had a pair of girls' panties with him that he left lying on the arm of John's couch and told me, "These are for John. Tell him we're even now".

Wishbone's answer sends a shockwave through the courtroom. So much commotion is coming from the back of the courtroom that I turn my head around to look at the gallery. As I do, I glance to where the parents are sitting and see the anguish on their faces. Judge Hart quickly restores quiet as I thank Wishbone for his testimony before sitting down.

Larry Hargrove's testimony corroborates what Wishbone testified to while adding that Larry cleaned John's house that day and he never saw anyone's panties while he was cleaning.

The D.A.'s cross-examination of both Larry and Wishbone doesn't catch either one misrepresenting the truth in their testimony, so she quits trying and sits down.

Judge Hart looks at me and asks, "Mr. Harris do you have any other witnesses?"

"Yes, Your Honor, the defense calls Detective Fowler as a witness for the Defendant." I answer.

It is almost unheard of for a criminal defense attorney

to call the lead detective prosecuting his client as a witness. I know that Randy's testimony will shore up John's defense. After the Detectives' testimony, the Judge will have no choice but to rule in our favor and not allow Rebecca's panties to be used as evidence in a trial for the murder of these little girls.

I watch as Randy takes the stand and is sworn in. I know he is aware that the government can't prove its case against my client. I also know that he thinks I should convince John to plead out. He doesn't understand that John isn't going to plead guilty to anything. John is too smart. John knew when he killed the little girls that he would never be punished for their murders. He planned it all out and his plan was going to work - with my help.

Through the Detective's testimony I am able to establish that he is the lead detective on this case and that he developed John as a suspect on a hunch. That "hunch" resulted in Larry Hargrove voluntarily giving him Rebecca Springer's panties when he did the "knock and talk" at John's house.

I am certain that Randy's answers to my next questions will tilt the scales of lady justice in John's favor.

"Detective Fowler were there traces of unknown DNA on Rebecca's panties?"

Randy stares straight at me as he answers my question, "Yes counselor."

I continue, "And have you been able to determine whose DNA matches the unknown DNA at this time?"

Detective Fowler replies, "Based on a tip from you, we obtained a search warrant for Bobby Meyers' apartment."

"Were you able to get a sample of Bobby Meyers' DNA during the course of your search of his apartment?" I ask.

"Yes" he replies curtly.

"Isn't it true that when Bobby Meyers' DNA was tested, it matched the unknown DNA found on Rebecca's panties?" I ask.

"Yes", he answers.

"Detective Fowler isn't it true that you found additional evidence that is relevant to John's defense when you searched Bobby Meyers' apartment?"

Randy answers me without breaking his stare, "You know exactly what we found counselor. We found a large collection of young girls' panties at Mr. Meyers apartment. A DNA analysis found no trace of any of the three victims on those panties though."

"It's also true you can't find Bobby Meyers, Detective Fowler, even though you looked for him?" I ask Randy.

He gives me a one-word answer, "Yes."

I have one last question for Randy. My question isn't to elicit any new facts that will help me in John's defense. My question is meant to emphasize the points I have already made. I want Judge Hart to concentrate on his reply when it is time for her to determine John's fate.

I take a deep breath and I ask Randy, "Detective let me get this straight. It's my understanding that the only evidence you have here today connecting John Lester to the murders of all three girls is Rebecca Springer's panties. Panties that were never in my client's possession. You don't have my client's DNA on the panties, but you do have DNA on them that match the DNA of Bobby Meyers. Further, Bobby Meyers had motive to frame John Lester, not to mention the fact that you found a collection of young girls' panties stashed in Bobby Meyer's apartment. Are those facts correct Detective Fowler?"

"Yes." Randy answers.

I thank Randy for his testimony and sit down next to John. Lindsey's cross examination of Randy doesn't take the sting out of the harm done to the government's case.

My closing argument points out the facts. The law makes it clear that allowing the government to use Rebecca's panties as evidence to convict John would be unfair. Lindsey's argument is feeble and unconvincing.

Judge Hart wastes no time giving her decision regarding my Motion.

The courtroom remains dead quiet as she declares in a loud clear voice, "The Court has heard the testimony of the witnesses and it is convinced that there is no reasonable nexus between the defendant, John Lester, and the panties found at his house. The Court finds the defendant's Motion to Suppress well taken and finds in favor of the defendant. The Court further finds that the only evidence the State has linking John Lester to the murders of these three children is the panties in question. Therefore, the court hereby dismisses all charges against the defendant at this time. Mr. Lester, you are free to go as soon as the Sheriff can process you out. That is the final ruling of the Court."

Judge Hart then bangs her gavel one last time before she leaves through the door to her chambers.

The whole time the Judge is announcing her decision, I keep my eyes glued on John. I want to make certain that he honors his pledge and does not bother the parents of the girls. He does honor his pledge. He looks straight ahead and barely moves his head while the Judge is offering her ruling. He knows I am staring at him and why. I keep my eyes on him as he is guided out of the courtroom by the guards.

Once John leaves the courtroom, I turn to find the reporters scrambling to get a quote from either Lindsey, Randy or me. I push my way through the reporters to Dorothy, Karen and Mrs. Lester. John's mother is beaming with joy while Dorothy and Karen are emotionless. Mrs. Lester grabs me and hugs my neck while profusely thanking me for saving her precious son's life. I tell her that I was just doing my job and she doesn't have to thank me.

I turn my attention to Dorothy to see if I can gauge her feelings. She looks at me with a faint smile on her face and winks. That isn't the reaction I am expecting from Dorothy. I'm not sure how to take it. Explanations will have to wait until later. Right now, I want to get the three of them out of here before the reporters start pestering them. I usher all three to the elevator doors and see them safely on their way before I turn to face the reporters.

I deal with the reporters and I notice Randy standing next to the courtroom door. It is obvious that he is waiting to speak to me.

I walk over until Randy and I are facing each other.
He asks me, "What are you going to do now William?"

CHAPTER 54

John has been free for close to two weeks now. He underestimated the amount of media coverage he would get after he was released from jail. Reporters were waiting to interview him as soon as he walked out. A few reporters even camped out in front of his house for the first few days once he got home.

To avoid the media, and being followed by Detective Fowler, he traveled to Memphis. The trip served several purposes: it gave him time to think and plan his next move.

He is restless. He wants to kill again... soon. He knows he has to take his time and be extremely careful before he can kill again. The memories of torturing and killing those three little whores had helped sustain his time locked up. He fantasized and relived the anguish he caused when he slaughtered those girls.

John learned from his first three murders. He will be careful and use more caution the next time he kills. He knows it is too risky for him to kill while he is in the spotlight.

John does his homework to decide which country will most accommodate his hobby. El Salvador looks promising. The government is weak and the authorities can be bought off. There are gangs in El Salvador that he could associate with. Those gangs would bring him young girls for the right amount of money.

John is flush with cash. The $5,000.00 his sister gives him each week to stay away from their mother built up during the weeks he was in jail. He already bought his airline ticket to El Salvador. When he gets there, he plans on spending a few months cultivating the people he needs. He will find them to help facilitate his need to kill. He knows he will kill during his visit to El Salvador.

John finds sitting in a motel room waiting for the media attention to taper off boring. He calls an escort service to send a prostitute to his motel room his last night in Memphis. He wants to ease the boredom but doesn't plan to hurt the whore, unfortunately.

The escort, who calls herself Brandy, arrives at his motel room. John commands her to strip naked the minute she arrives. He sits in a chair with his back against the wall while she stands about three feet away from him. He watches while she takes off her clothes, one piece at a time. Watching the whore take off her clothes excites John.

As Brandy undresses for him, it reminds him of stripping those three little sluts naked before he tortured and killed them. The closer the whore comes to taking her panties off, the more aroused he becomes. As she finally takes her panties off, he can no longer contain his desire and he lunges for her. As the whore screams, a loud violent banging starts on the door.

At the same moment, a man starts yelling at the top of his lungs, "Open the fucking door or I will kick it down!"

John doesn't panic. He quickly sorts out the situation. The whore isn't hurt and he hasn't broken any laws. The best thing to do is let the meddlesome asshole on the other side of the door know he isn't needed.

When he walks over to the door, he opens it partially. He holds the door in front of him as he peeps around the side of the door. He plans to tell the asshole that everything is alright and to mind his own business. Before John can utter a word, the stranger pushes the door open, knocking John back into the room.

The stranger steps into the hotel room holding a gun in his hand, pointed towards the floor.

The stranger sees Brandy laying on the bed and asks her "You alright ma'am? Do I need to call the law?"

Brandy replies with a shaky voice, "Yeah, I'm ok. He didn't

hurt me, it just got out of hand - no need to call the law. I don't need any more trouble tonight. But if it's all right mister, I would like to leave with you."

The stranger looks at John and asks him "Is that going to be a problem?"

John is bewildered with the turn of events. It is hard for him to fathom how a good Samaritan, with a pistol, happened to be walking by when the whore screamed. To top it off, the stranger winds up in John's room with a gun in his hand. It really doesn't matter how the stranger interjected himself, he is involved now. The whore said what John wants to hear. Don't call the law. He doesn't need to be involved in any trouble with the police.

John looks at the stranger, shakes his head, and says, "No problem."

John is relieved when the prostitute and the stranger leave. Brandy doesn't even bother to put her clothes on. She quickly bundles her clothes in her arms and takes off with the stranger. John chucks the whole experience up to a "what the fuck just happened moment" and writes the whole thing off.

CHAPTER 55

John checks out of his motel room the next day in order to drive back to Nashville. He doesn't plan on going straight to his house. He doesn't want to take a chance on letting anyone know he is back in town. He wants to make sure he isn't followed tonight. His destination is his church...his sanctuary...in the woods where he keeps his trophies.

He never stops thinking about his secret place where Patsy's and Tammy's panties are on display for his eyes only. He yearns to get back to that cabin. He craves the touch and smell of the panties. The aroma on the dead girls' panties will drive him wild as he rubs the soft silky fabric across his face. He hopes he still smells the fear of those girls on them.

John knows tonight will be his last time to relish the touch and the smell of the little sluts' panties. He will have to destroy everything linking him to the three girls' murders tonight. The evidence at the farm will be easy to purge. A bonfire out back of the cabin will quickly obliterate all traces linking the dead girls to him.

A far more difficult problem he faces tonight is disposing of Bobby Meyers' body. He has done his homework and the best method is to burn the body beyond recognition. He has enough firewood at the cabin to have a fire that will obliterate all traces of a human body. The biggest hurdle he has to jump over is that bodies don't generally burn at the temperature of your average bonfire. The furnace in a crematorium burns at over 1000°c and even that takes about three hours to completely reduce a body to ash. He has enough wood that he can maintain a fire hot enough and long enough to guarantee the destruction of the body and the panties, he hopes.

By the time he gets back to Nashville, the sun is starting to set in the western sky. He parks his Mercedes at the shopping mall where he leaves it before accessing his trusty Ford Taurus. He always uses the Taurus to go to the farm or snatch a victim. He knows his car is ready. He keeps a charger on it at all times when it is stored. He knows that when he picks up the car, he might be in a hurry. The car will always be charged and ready to go. He doesn't have time to waste with a dead battery.

John walks the short distance from the shopping mall to the storage facility. It will take him a little more than an hour to finally see his church and he can barely contain his excitement.

John's drive to the farm prompts him to chuckle as he thinks about William Harris, the attorney. The man has the ability to terrify him and rekindle his fear of death. John hadn't been able to control William with intimidation. But he doesn't have to intimidate to control. John has controlled his attorney with the attorney's own honesty and devotion to his oath to obey the law. He played William perfectly. William managed John's case the way John planned. That is the reason John is free tonight. He thinks it is ironic that he is free to kill again, thanks to William. He will think of his attorney the next time he kills. Actually, every time he kills, John will think of William and smile.

His drive from Nashville to the farm in Wilson County, is agonizingly slow. He smiles, as he passes through the small town of Statesville on the lonely and deserted country road. He is in a state of excited frenzy as he exits the country road onto the driveway leading to his cabin.

He finds the cabin intact and is pleased there isn't a foul odor emanating from Bobby's dead body. Bobby's carcass has been stashed in the shed behind the cabin since before he went to jail.

He wastes little time entering the cabin and lighting the kerosene lamp sitting on a table next to the entrance. The light from the lamp casts a dim glow that allows John to survey the room. Nothing has changed in the months he has been away.

John's mind isn't focused on anything but the back room where his church, with his trophies, is waiting.

He holds the kerosene lamp in one hand as he walks through the house. When he opens the door and steps inside, the warm glow from the lamp lights the room. He immediately looks toward the back of the room where he has his altar set up. The altar consists of a table pushed against the wall with photographs taken from the newspapers of Patsy and Tammy. Those photographs are framed and sitting on top of the table, facing the room. John also has Polaroids he took of the girls' bodies when he was finished torturing them. He likes the fact that they were still alive when he took the pictures. John has those special photos framed and hanging on the wall. The girls' panties are on little hooks attached to the frames.

The sight of those panties gives John an instant erection. He slowly closes the distance from the door to his altar, stops and shuts his eyes. He leans his head back while slipping his hand down into his pants to touch his growing erection.

He places the kerosene lamp down and undoes his belt and zipper. He lets his pants slide down his legs. With his free hand, he reaches out and begins rubbing the fabric of one of the girl's panties between his fingers while stroking himself. John is startled by the sound of the door behind him opening.

He turns at the noise, in time to see William and the stranger from the Memphis motel room, coming through the door. The stranger follows William as they enter the room. Both are holding large black pistols, pointed directly at him. He is terrified again.

His terror shows in his voice as he asks in a rush, "What are you doing here? How did you find this place? Who is he?"

CHAPTER 56

I wasn't sure what I would find when I opened the door in front of me. I damn sure didn't expect to find John standing there with his pants down around his ankles, holding his dick in his hand. If the scene before us wasn't so disturbing, Dakota and I would be laughing out loud. But we are both sickened.

I hear John's questions. I recall him telling me that there were crimes and details that I didn't need to know to effectively represent him. I find the tables reversed. I've committed crimes to find John and this place that I have no interest in telling him about. I don't need to tell him anything to accomplish what I am here to do.

He doesn't need to know that I spoke with Randy after Judge Hart ruled in John's favor.

After the hearing, when Randy asked me what I was going to do now, my response to Randy was short. "I need a throw-away."

Randy knew exactly what I meant. We didn't need to talk about it.

John doesn't need to know that I met Randy at my office later that day and he gave me the gun I'm pointing at John now.

He doesn't need to know that I gave Randy the tracking device to put on John's Mercedes before it was released from the impound lot.

He doesn't need to know that Randy advised me of the twenty-one-foot rule. The rule that is taught in the police academy warning all fresh-faced cadets not to let a threatening offender get within twenty-one-feet before shooting. If they get closer than that you lose the advantage of a weapon.

He doesn't need to know that the man standing behind me is my best friend, Dakota. John doesn't need to know that Dakota has been following him since they released him from jail. Dakota watched the prostitute enter John's room in Memphis and was standing right outside the door when she screamed.

He doesn't need to know that Dakota was never going to allow him to hurt someone or kill anyone ever again.

He doesn't need to know that Dakota and I were following his Mercedes when he drove to the mall tonight.

He doesn't need to know that we saw him leave his car and walk to the storage unit to retrieve the white Ford Taurus, or that we followed him to Wilson County to the turn off to the cabin.

Most of all, John doesn't need to know that my commitment to Maria compelled me to tell her I was going to kill him if Judge Hart cut him loose.

Maria's response had been what I expected when she told me, "Kill El Diablo - just don't get caught."

John doesn't need to know that I am going to fulfill both of those requests tonight.

So, when John asks what I am doing here, how I found him and who Dakota is, I simply say, "That's none of your fucking business."

CHAPTER 57

*J*ohn is taking deep breaths through his nostrils - clearing his head so he can think. He is sure that William isn't here to kill him. He is certain he isn't going to die tonight. William won't kill him. William has too much on the line. John might go back to jail but at least he isn't going to die tonight.

John is sure that he will live. However, he is resigned to the fact that he is going back to jail when he throws up his hands and says, "Ok counselor, you've got me. But I promise you that I'll beat this. I'll be back out hunting before you know it. My mother will hire a team of lawyers to get me off. You can bet on that."

"You're not going back to jail," William responds.

John's shit-eating grin disappears completely when William says that. Now William has a shit-eating grin of his own.

John hears William and that can only mean one thing. William isn't going to take him back to jail. John's terror returns. He is so scared he pisses and shits himself.

Dakota is about to vomit from the smell and tells William, "Fuck! Let's get this over with. This guy is disgusting. I can't even stand to be in here. If you don't shoot that stinky motherfucker, I will."

Out of desperation, John begins to beg and cry at the same time. "Please let me live. You promised me that if I left the parents of those girls alone you wouldn't kill me. You're a man of honor. You told me you always keep your promises. You promised!!"

The last thought that runs through John's mind is that he

is headed for that dark place he fears, which can only be Hell.

The last four words John hears before a bullet tears through his brain is William saying, "I lied. Things change."

EPILOGUE

It's a cold Winter day and Detective Randy Fowler is headed to Wilson County on an anonymous tip he received about John Lester. Randy has called to get an officer from the Wilson County Sheriff's Office to meet him at a farm located in Statesville. He is relieved that he will finally be able to give the parents of Tammy Mars, Patsy Oakley and Rebecca Springer closure. They need to hear that John Lester is dead.

Randy already knows there is plenty of evidence to show the world that John Lester murdered the girls. He is also certain he will find the rotting body of Bobby Meyers at the cabin. He isn't interested in solving the murder of this bastard, John Lester. He already knows the tip came from a burner phone and there's no way to trace it. He wants to see the sick son of a bitch's corpse. If Lieutenant Tim Harding wants to get involved, that's up to him. But as far as Detective Randy Fowler is concerned the case belongs to Wilson County. It doesn't bother him because he knows the case will never be solved.

ABOUT THE AUTHOR:

Michie Gibson (Michie is pronounced "Mickey" like the mouse) lives in Tennessee, married and has two grown sons. He was a bouncer for ten years before becoming an attorney and had several brushes with the law. He has been practicing law in Nashville for over 30 years. He has handled hundreds of criminal cases and several death penalty cases.

Michie has taken his life experiences, and a knack for story telling, to weave a yarn that he hopes will keep you guessing with characters that you will either love or hate. Michie likes to call himself a "master bullshitter" and in this first novel, William Harris' story contains enough facts, with a lot of fiction added in to render a tale that he hopes will keep you turning pages.

A NOTE FROM THE AUTHOR:

I hope you enjoyed this book and would be grateful if you would take a minute out of your day to leave a short review on Amazon.

If you would like to keep up with future happenings, please visit my author web-site: www.michiegibson.com

Like the Michie Gibson author pages on:

Facebook http://www.facebook.com/ michiegibsonauthor

Instagram http://www.instagram.com/ michiegibsonauthor

Follow me on Amazon

http://amazon.com/author/michiegibson

Made in the USA
Lexington, KY
18 August 2019